THE LAST ENEMY

A TIME TRAVELLER'S BEST FRIEND: BOOK THREE

W.R. GINGELL

In memoriam:
my sanity

EMERGENCY HAT

Sergeant Gormley was expecting a Very Busy Day. In preparation for that day, he had gone to bed last night at exactly 10:00 Local Relative Time, expecting to wake again at exactly 06:00 LRT and thus achieve the optimal eight hours of sleep. From then, if he had been the type of person to make detailed plans, he would have penned out a simple itinerary: 06:00—wake, shower. 06:30—having showered, breakfast. 07:30—report for duty to the outbound ship that was taking him and a few of his men to collect evidence from a small fixed orbit fuel station that was one of a group orbiting Fifth World's moon.

Evidence collection was not in Sergeant Gormley's wheelhouse, nor did he feel comfortable leaving the fixed orbit evidence station that slowly circled Fourth World, but he had been ordered to go, and go he would. He would merely make sure to fortify himself against the rigors of the coming day by sleeping appropriately.

So when he was woken instead at 05:45 LRT, Sergeant Gormley felt a sense of betrayal toward his body, which had never before so served him. Nor did he dare to roll over and try to sleep again for those lost fifteen minutes, because if he couldn't trust his body to wake him at the exact time today, he certainly couldn't trust it not to oversleep itself.

Instead, he stared grimly at his dark ceiling, and wondered if it was just the grogginess of that lost fifteen minutes that made him see things on the ceiling.

Only then the ceiling said, "You awake or wot?"

Sergeant Gormley yelped and tumbled away as quickly as a man of his bulk could do, alighting on his feet beside his bed and leaping backward from there with his weapon in his hand and pointed at the mass of shadows on his ceiling that was now...gone.

"Reckon you'd know better by now," said the same sharp voice in a conversational manner, from behind him.

The Sergeant whipped around, but his weapon was already sinking—much like his heart. He knew that pinched little voice;

he also knew the little person it belonged to, and the habit that child had of wriggling through any possible crawl space and quite a few that weren't possible.

"Flamin' rude!" said the child now in front of him, looking accusingly at him through a black fringe that was just a bit longer than usual but just as ragged as last time he'd seen it, the edges of her bob likewise longer than usual. Her light armoured stockings hung loosely on her skinny legs, which were visible through a small ladder that must have been achieved via something in the region of a light discharge weapon or something even heavier. They had been like that last time he saw her, too; he wondered why she still wore them. Over the stockings, she wore a flowered dress that was likewise too large, and a knitted jumper that fit her just slightly better than the last one he'd seen her in.

She added, "I come visit you and you point yer zapper at me!"

"I didn't ask you to come visit me," pointed out the sergeant, rather hopelessly. "And if it comes to that—"

That made her grin, which worried him.

"Yeah, but ain't it fun!"

"Not usually," he said. "Were you crawling around in the vents again?"

"Close enough," she said, which was even more worrying. If it was just the vents, he could have fixed that up right and tight, but Kez had other ways of getting around that were quite frankly impossible; moreover, to him it sounded as though she was trying to soothe him.

He asked painedly, "What do you want?"

"Came to give you a present," she said.

"No, thank you," said Sergeant Gormley. She had given him a lunchbox with explosive in it once, and he had been wary of gifts ever since.

"You'll like it."

"I bet I won't."

"Got a real 'ang dog attitude, ain't you?" she said. "Well, suit yourself, but I reckon you'll regret it if you don't take it."

And there it was. Sergeant Gormley very much disliked everything he had yet received from Kez—up to and including several knocks on the head—but he was quite well aware that he would have liked still less the things that would have happened if he had not been the recipient of said gratuities.

He sighed; a big, deep thing that could only be achieved by someone with a chest the size of the sergeant, and Kez, apparently taking that for assent, fished in the pocket of her flowered dress and pulled out a fat square of material.

She tossed it at the sergeant and he caught it, only to find himself unfolding a fabric hat of the sort that was still worn occasionally by armed forces on principally human-occupied planets.

"What's this?" Sergeant Gormley asked. He felt rather faint and completely out of his depth, which was nothing unusual when it came to dealing with Kez. He had an awful presentiment that Something was About to Happen, and he *very much didn't want* for Something to Happen.

"Emergency 'at," Kez told him, grinning that awful, gleeful grin at him. "For when stuff goes wrong, see? When everyfink goes wrong, pop that on yer noggin."

"What will it do?"

She looked at him suspiciously. "You drunk?"

Sergeant Gormley, who had never yet taken the smallest drop of alcohol on the job, much less at 05:45 before work, protested, "What? no!"

"It's an *'at*," Kez said to him, slowly and clearly. "It don't *do* nuffink. You *wears* it."

"I know it's a—can't I speak to Marx?"

Kez's crabbed little face grew pinched and stormy. "No, you can't! Uncle Cheng's sorted that out an' I'm gunna kick 'im in the shins fer it. Just flamin' do as you're told."

"Are you—are you alone?" he asked her tentatively. Kez was

certainly feral, but she was usually at least a hard, certain kind of feral; in Sergeant Gormley's far from expert opinion, she had achieved a kind of security with the short, angry man she travelled with, and if Marx wasn't inclined to be less angry with her around, at least that anger had a very narrow focus. In a strange way, they seemed to do each other good.

Today's Kez was more feral and brittle, and the sergeant wasn't at all sure he wouldn't end up being bitten if he didn't tread carefully.

Her eyes very shiny, Kez said vehemently, "You gotta *wait*! Ain't nobody seein' Marx until I do! Everyfink's gorn wrong and I'm tryin' to *fix* it so you better do what you're told!"

"Why—why should everything go wrong?" he asked, rather weakly. He was afraid to ask, because if he asked, she would tell him, and then Sergeant Gormley would have to do something about it. He was very well aware that he didn't have the kind of nerves required to live life as Kez and Marx lived it, and he would very much prefer not to get caught up with them at all. "What's supposed to happen?"

"That's the point, innit?" she muttered darkly, as if to herself. "Stuff wot's s'posed to 'appen."

If he had before been afraid that she would tell him what she was up to, Sergeant Gormley now began to be afraid that she would immediately flit off and leave him with the heavy weight of something to be done without giving him the means of doing something about it until it was too late, and it had happened.

"Yes, but you said you want me to stop it. What is it you want me to do? What's going to happen?"

"All you gotta do is stop it 'appenin'," she said. "Don't matter 'ow, so long as you get it done."

Sergeant Gormley sat down on the bed, gripping her shoulder comfortingly, and said in his most kindly tone, "I know that you *think* you're explaining it. But if you want me to stop something, you'll have to tell me exactly what it is you want me to stop."

Kez stared at him for a brief, furious moment, then at the large, comforting hand that entirely swallowed up her shoulder, and he saw the flash of feral rage in her eyes just a moment too late to pull his right shin out of reach of her steel-capped boots.

Having thoroughly kicked that shin and released herself from his hand in one shot, Kez retreated back across the room in the flicker of an eyelid. Sergeant Gormley was quite sure she hadn't walked.

Clutching his shin, he tried to be grateful that she hadn't bitten off one of his fingers, as he had momentarily been afraid that she might. This version of Kez was feral and scared and angry; raging alone and hitting out in all directions without caring who got hurt. Who had done this to her—the Uncle Cheng she had mentioned?

His voice was more breathless than kindly as he said, "I need to know what to look out for if you want my help."

Her face pinched in a bit more, and her eyes grew black. "Ain't your business," she said. "You just do what you gotta do, yeah?"

"Yes, but I don't know what it is you want me to do!"

"You gotta stop something from 'appenin'."

"All right, but what something?"

Her eyes became even more pebbly. "Can't tell you what. Not 'zactly."

"Can you tell me where? Can you tell me why?"

"You're goin' on a bit of a trip today, ain't you? That's when it'll 'appen. You gotta stop everyone from dyin', see? If they dies, then—then—"

Sergeant Gormley said, very gently, "What happens if I can't save everyone?"

"Summink real bad," she said quietly. "If they dies, summink real bad 'appens to me, and then summink real bad 'appens to the universe."

"If I stop it?" he asked apprehensively. He had never been quite sure of where Kez and Marx's loyalties lay, other than to themselves; but then, he had never seen Kez quite this scared and feral, either. "What happens then?"

"Nuffink," she said. "An' that's what we want to 'appen."

She disappeared without warning and then reappeared briefly in a flutter of floral print, to stab a small finger at him violently. "In case of emergencies, see? Use yer 'at."

Sergeant Gormley still desperately wished to know exactly what the hat would do in an emergency to fix the situation; he did not consider it overreaching to want to know what situation was likely to occur, either. In fact, he was left in a situation of general *unknowing* that would have pleased him greatly if it wasn't for the fact that he knew there was *something* he ought to know. Sergeant Gormley preferred not to know what he shouldn't know, but he was quite as settled in his preference to know everything if he *had* to know something.

He must save everyone—but exactly where was it that everyone was going to be in danger? And what was it that was going to happen? When? How was he to save the *everyone* Kez had mentioned if he didn't know what he was doing? What if he saved only some of those in danger? He remembered Kez's strained face, and his jaw set: he mustn't let any of them die, or something—something so bad that even Kez couldn't say it— would happen. It was evident that something bad had already happened, or Kez wouldn't be alone. What had happened there, he didn't know, and he would almost rather not know. Sergeant Gormley was a man who preferred not to have too many thoughts wandering around in his head to disturb him. It prevented him from being able to do what needed to be done; and he was quite sure that whatever it was he had to do, he would need to be as little distracted as possible in order to get it done.

Several things occurred to Sergeant Gormley as he ate his breakfast. Several more did not. For instance, it did not occur to him that if he simply failed to report for duty, or applied to have his men taken off today's roster, he could avoid the distinct possibility of dying horribly today. It didn't occur to him that if he reported the appearance of a wanted criminal to the Time Corp, they would take care of both Kez herself and the prospective interference with a fixed orbit fuel station.

It *did* occur to him that if Kez was without Marx, it was better for all concerned if he did what she asked him to do. Kez with Marx was unpredictable, savage, and inclined to bite, but anecdotally, Kez without Marx was frightened, savage, and inclined to cause the implosion of whole worlds. And if there was a question of people dying and worlds imploding, there really wasn't any other choice: Sergeant Gormley would do what he was told, even if he was being told what to do by a minor with rage issues and a single, incoherent directive.

He would have done so anyway, of course, but it did leave him with an added incentive to make sure that he did the job *well*.

He found himself jumpier than he liked as he boarded the transport skip with seven of his men. It was bad enough to be leaving the station to collect evidence like a beat sergeant; to be walking into goodness knew what and charged with saving everyone on the station from certain death was very nearly too much for his nerves. Sergeant Gormley liked following orders, but he liked his orders to make sense, and he liked having someone above him to take the blame if things went wrong.

Still, the sergeant was well respected these days, and it wouldn't do to startle too visibly whenever one of his men unexpectedly addressed him, so he pulled himself together and began to think of all the things that could possibly go wrong on a fixed-orbit fuel repository. The first thing, of course, was the possibility of accidental explosion; something that could happen naturally on a fuel station if someone didn't observe all the safety protocols. Sergeant Gormley was gloomily sure that anything involving Kez and Marx wouldn't be as simple as an accident, but it was a possibility. Secondly, it was possible that someone wanted to make a statement by ostentatiously blowing up a station and all hands on deck; it would certainly be spectacular, and the amount of staff who would be lost was significant.

Barring that, the only other option seemed to be the possibility of war beginning, and Sergeant Gormley refused to think about such a possibility at all. He refused to allow it to exist, and therefore turned his mind toward the more likely of his two options instead.

If Kez and Marx were involved, it was unlikely that his mission pertained to anything so purposeless as an accidental explosion on a fuel station: no, it was far more likely that someone was deliberately trying to blow up the station, and the sooner he discovered why, the closer he would be to finding out who was trying to do such a thing, and stopping it in time.

"Who else is coming to the station today?" he asked his second in command as they stepped into the cargo deck, still shivering from the cold blast of airy disinfectant at entry and decontamination.

The corporal was new to him; a thin lad who looked like he'd just graduated school. Still, he was quick with his work and took only a moment to log into the station's system.

"Just us, sir, and two small dockings to refuel. They're pretty quiet here."

"There are a lot of staff here for a day as quiet as that," the sergeant observed. There would be more people up on the next level, the passenger deck, but not too many more. "Do they usually have days with *nothing* happening?"

"They train new fuel monkeys here," the boy explained, and looked at him with a mixture of curiosity and respect that Sergeant Gormley still wasn't quite used to from his men, despite the popularity he had recently gained. "Is there something wrong, sir?"

"Yes," said the Sergeant, his gaze running over the staff who were de-greasing the vents on one side of the vast deck, and the ones who were repairing one of the airlock hatches that led to space and not much else. "But I don't know what, yet. What are the two dockings?"

"One's a Time Corp sloop that just came back from recon at Fourth World and needs a top-up to get to home base; the other's a privately owned cargo-runner."

"What's the paperwork look like?" Sergeant Gormley asked. He didn't trust privately owned cargo-running ships—nor, to his great surprise at the discovery, did he particularly trust the Time Corp fully any longer.

"For the cargo-runner?"

"For both," said the sergeant, a little grimly. "And did the cargo-runner drop anything, or is it just picking up fuel?"

The corporal made a few swipes and tapped the screen twice. "First glance, everything looks fine. They've both completed a docking bill that shows where they're coming from, and they've both submitted logs to prove where they've been. The sloop hasn't allowed itself to be connected to the main system, but the cargo-runner didn't put up a fuss; they dropped some supplies here for the crew this morning...and it looks like they've just left."

"It's not unusual for Time Corp to skip out on the connection," the sergeant said slowly. There was sensitive information on more than one Time Corp vessel, and there were risks inherent in connecting to another online system. Not connecting meant that you had to approve everything the other side did to your ship manually, but it also decreased the likelihood of anyone infiltrating your ship's system.

"Not unusual," agreed the corporal. He took another look at his sergeant and added, "So why are you still suspicious, sir?"

"That's the point," said the sergeant gloomily. "I don't know. Prod at the cargo-runner's records a bit more, there's a good lad: the rest of you get going with the evidence collection. I'm going to take a walk up to the passenger deck and swap greetings with the TC sloop."

"I can work while I walk, sir," the boy said eagerly, as his other men saluted and headed off in search of their evidence. "I think I could be useful to you."

"Do you?" asked Sergeant Gormley, fascinated. He didn't know what he was doing or what he was looking for; he wasn't sure *he* could be useful. Nor was he used to being looked at with quite the amount of eagerness that the corporal was looking at him. He hated to think that he would have to either live up to that eagerness or bitterly disappoint it. "I suppose you'd better come along, then."

Fortunately for Sergeant Gormley's already frazzled nerves, the boy could and did walk as he worked, even when climbing up through the gangway. He seemed to have some sort of sixth sense for what was around him, and avoided people and obstacles alike while tapping away at his little console.

When they drew nearer to the place where the Time Corp sloop was docked, however, the boy's footsteps seemed to slow.

"You said you wanted to talk with the commanding officer of the *Resilient*, didn't you sir?"

"If that's the *Resilient*," said Sergeant Gormley, pointing at the maxiplex windows, through which part of the Time Corp sloop hull could be seen, "then yes."

"Yes, sir," said the corporal, tapping again at his little screen. "Only I don't seem to be able to raise anyone. I think they're ignoring me."

Sergeant Gormley was about to give his opinion on members of the Time Corp who thought themselves above their counterparts in the WAOF, but his comm blinked at him.

"We've got the evidence, sir," said one of his men, over the comm. "But some of it is a bit wilted—the plant matter, that is. It might be a bit hard to preserve it properly. Should we try to preserve a few specimens rather than the whole lot?"

Sergeant Gormley frowned. The evidence that they needed to collect had been back down on the cargo deck, which was usually pretty well temperature-controlled due to the cooling needed for the reception and output of some of the more volatile types of fuel. Under normal circumstances, plant matter should have been well and truly healthy.

He hesitated, then said, "Do a temperature check."

He might not have ordered it on any other day. He liked to think he would have, but on most days, a little extra nosing around was all the difference between getting back to the station in time for the best of what was in the mess hall, or missing out.

Today, however, was different.

Today, a very angry little girl was depending on him to make sure that something that wasn't meant to happen, didn't happen.

And today, there was someone in a very poor representation of a Time Corp uniform messing with the interface outside the hatch where the *Resilient* was docked.

"You there!" yelled Sergeant Gormley, lurching forward into the heavy, juggernaut run that had scared many a malefactor into running for it by pure instinct.

The figure was not one of that kind: instead, it stayed where it was, typing furiously, intently, until he was just a few metres away. Then it slapped shut the hatch and ran for it.

"I've got him, sir!" yelled the corporal, sprinting past the sergeant with all the vigour of his youth.

Sergeant Gormley stopped by the hatch in some relief, sweating, and hoped that he could understand enough of the systems to be able to see what the man had been doing. Luckily for him, the language was set to Universal and seemed to have been designed with people of Sergeant Gormley's ilk in mind: that is, it was delightfully simple.

The sign-in log was the first thing he accessed, but it had been cleared just moments before; no doubt the final thing the malefactor had done before being caught. Sergeant Gormley heaved a huge sigh of discouragement, and thought very hard. What could someone have been trying to get at from a standard portal on the passenger deck of a fuel station? Certainly someone could access all the systems if they had the appropriate credentials, but it wasn't likely for persons unknown to have those kind of credentials. Especially the kind of persons unknown who ran at the first sign of trouble instead of sticking around to try and face it out.

If they did have that kind of access, someone must have given it to them.

Alarmed, Sergeant Gormley tried to enter the change logs. If the runner had access to the sort of things he oughtn't to, anything he had tried to do in the system should be listed in the change logs.

Access denied popped up on the screen. Below it, *System Password Reset* blinked steadily at the sergeant, turning the sweat cold on his brow. If they had reset the system password as well as changing stars knew what on the system, Sergeant Gormley was not sure what he could do.

He stopped to think again, laboriously, and a sparkling idea lit in his mind. Exiting the change logs, Sergeant Gormley accessed the last day's worth of system searches instead. A list flashed up on the screen, ten lines deep: five of them from the last half hour.

"Sir," said a voice on his comms, as he did so. "The cargo deck—it's—the temperature is ten degrees above recommended down here, and someone has broken the thermostat control to keep it that way."

"I see," said Sergeant Gormley, who could think of only a few reasons why that might be happening, none of which were heartening. "Gather all the evidence you can; take specimens and take anything you can fit in your kits and in your pockets. One of you scout around the cargo deck."

"Yes sir," said the comm. "What are we looking for?"

"Explosive," Sergeant Gormley said grimly, because between the system searches he could see and the temperature controls being so far above what they ought to be, he had a pretty good idea what the Time Corp pretender had been up to.

There was a beat of silence. "Sir?"

"Look for explosive!" barked the sergeant, scanning the search logs once more, then pulling up the cargo lists. "The cargo runner dropped something earlier today, and we just had a runner in fake Time Corp kit fiddling with the system to find out where it was kept. Someone also accessed the hatch locks— I'd guess they were looking for a way to get it in safely. If we're lucky, we can get to whatever explosive was left before they arm it."

"If they've got temperature control on it, it's probably already armed, sir," said one of his men. "I mean, it'll be decreasing in stability as it goes, and I bet they're really sure about how quickly it destabilises at this temperature, too."

Sergeant Gormley wiped his brow with one ham-like hand that shook a bit. "Look for time stamps," he said. "Anything from this morning: anything the size of a small pallet. And one of you look for a way to lower the temperature on the cargo deck."

He went back to the portal, desperately trying to make more sense of what he was looking at. The cargo he now suspected to be explosive had been on board since before the Time Corp sloop logged in: had been there, in fact, since the earlier docking of the cargo-runner, which had brought it. Why had the fake Time Corp runner first searched to make sure it was there, then checked on the outer hatches in the system? Surely that was something that should have been done much earlier, to see if there was another way of getting the explosives on board? Why, in fact, was someone pretending to be Time Corp when the real Time Corp was nearby, and *why wasn't anyone from the Resilient answering comms*?

Sergeant Gormley closed off the portal and broke into a trot once again, heading for the gangway that led back down to the cargo deck. "Corporal, do you have the runner?"

His corporal, panting, came on the line to say, "He killed himself, sir."

"He what?" asked the sergeant blankly.

"He *killed* himself," the boy said again, bitterly. "I tried to get him to spit it out and he wouldn't."

"Good lad," said Sergeant Gormley, barrelling down the gangway and startling passing staff. "No need to worry; you did what you could. Can you clean it up?"

"Yes, sir."

Sergeant Gormley, jogging across the cargo dock, found his men clustered around a small pallet that barely came to his knee. If it was lacking in size, it wasn't lacking in menace: a vague yellow discolouration seemed to hang over the whole.

"Report!" he barked.

"It's explosive, sir; Geumbang. Morliss estimates that we've got about twenty minutes before it goes, with the state it's in."

"Can we vent cooler air—"

Morliss was already shaking his head, so Sergeant Gormley turned directly to him. "What about it, Morliss?"

"My brother-in-law works with this stuff, sir. It's already giving off gas: you can't reverse the amount of degradation, and you can't stop it from keeping *on* degrading. It'll blow no matter what we do."

"Can we get it off the deck?"

"No, sir. We try to move it and *boom*. I've seen what happens when you try to shift it with a disintegrator, too; it's not pretty, sir. The explosion gets *really* big."

There was a moment of silence in which Sergeant Gormley was quite certain his men could hear him sweating.

One of them said, after another moment, "What now, sir?"

"Evacuate," said Sergeant Gormley.

"Sir, they're Fifth Worlders, and there's no one in authority on deck."

"I know," the sergeant said, on a groan. Fifth Worlders in crisis milled like bees without a queen to direct them.

"It'll be pandemonium!"

"Better than a slaughterhouse," said the sergeant grimly, and touched his comms button. Better get the station officials to direct this lot if they wanted to save anyone today. "Control Room. Control Room. Sergeant Gormley of the WAOF cutting in: you'll need to evacuate."

There was no reply.

To his men, he said, "You four, get to the upper deck and be ready to direct the evacuation up there."

They said a brisk *yes sir* and left.

More sharply, Sergeant Gormley said into his comms, "Station Control Room. Do you copy? There are explosives in the cargo dock. You need to start evacuation protocols."

A breathless voice answered him. "They've beggared off, sir!"

"Corporal? What are you doing in the Control Room?"

"Had a suspicion, sir."

"Well done, Corporal. They've run off?"

"All of them, sir. I've initiated the evacuation protocols."

Overhead, sirens began to wail: a series of lights lit up on the decking, pointing to the closest exits. "Good man. Hopefully this lot knows how to use an emergency exit."

To his relief, they did. The crowd split into two, surging toward the two escape pod exits, and milled at each one, never seeming to grow smaller, though each half of the crowd did seem to grow more frantic.

"Why aren't they getting out?" Sergeant Gormley asked the two officers still flanking him, frowning. "Go check on the hatches; open them manually if you have to. Get everyone onboard the escape pods and come back when you're done. Each of you to a side."

They did as they were told, threading through the crowd, and Sergeant Gormley forged his way through to the airlocks instead. There was something uniform and not quite right about them: it wasn't until he was closer that he realised that the unfamiliar uniformity of them had to do with the serried ranks of plastic explosive that had been dotted across every join and every potential weakness in the hatches.

Sergeant Gormley's heart sank as he gazed at the orderliness of it. When had that been done? He remembered someone working on the hatches, but he had assumed it to be a repair person. Each line of explosive ended in a small, tidy detonator that was far too small for the sergeant to think about removing, even if he had had the stomach to do it.

He couldn't see a timer on them, but if he had had a guess, he would have guessed that they were set to explode just before the main load, maximising panic and preventing any chance of disarming the main load while everyone tried to stabilise the airlocks before they gave way to pressure.

"Sir, you should see this," said one of his men, appearing by his side again.

Sergeant Gormley followed the man across the deck, wading into the seething panic closest to the emergency exits and wishing that his own brain was seething a little less.

It was a tight squeeze close to the emergency exits, but once there, the sergeant found himself even more breathless than he ought to have been.

The hatches were locked. Not only were they locked via the main system, they were physically locked from the other side. Nor, if his straining eyes were to be trusted as he peered through the glassy window into the area that ought to have led to the escape pod but was worryingly dark, were there escape pods attached to the station any longer.

And the sergeant finally understood. The searches he had seen in the console hadn't been the attempts of persons unknown to open the airlocks and allow in an unknown craft. No; the explosives had already been onboard. The Time Corp pretender hadn't been trying to blow anything up: he had been trying to prevent anyone from escaping from the station once the trouble began. He had known about the attack, and he had been determined that no one should escape it.

Sergeant Gormley began to sweat again. He was not good at swift movement of the brain; his forte was in stolidly obeying orders and staying exactly where he was told to stay. He had thwarted many a criminal by doing exactly that, but in this case, where the foe was faceless and already several moves ahead of him, the sergeant had no idea of where to turn.

Nor, it seemed, did the people aboard the fixed-orbit station: Fifth Worlders milled everywhere, a surging, whirling mass that pushed one way and then another in search of somewhere safe to go, or at least some potential exit.

"Corporal," he said to his comm, huskily. "Can you get aboard the Time Corp sloop?"

"Yes sir," came the answer, swiftly.

Sergeant Gormley wouldn't have been surprised to find that the boy was already halfway there.

"What do you want me to tell them, sir? If they're still there, that is."

"Tell them that you're commandeering the sloop."

"*Yes*, sir!"

Sergeant Gormley had a truly impressive bellow, and hitherto he had been able to accomplish all he needed to accomplish upon commencement of the same. This time, he was singularly unsuccessful, his roar lost in the turbulent rumble of the crowd, and he was left with the frustration of knowing exactly what needed to be done without any idea of how to achieve it.

"I don't think it's going to work, sir!" yelled one of his officers through the comms, from across the room. "And those airlocks—!"

"Get the gangway open," the sergeant said. "Up to the passenger deck: manually, if you have to. They'll come rushing as soon as they see it open. We can still get them up on the passenger deck and herd them toward the sloop, even if we can't use the escape pods. You four up on deck—get ready to receive refugees: direct 'em toward the Time Corp sloop if you can."

Rather to his relief, he was correct: as soon as the flashing light above the entrance signalled that the gangway was clear, there was a surge toward it; then a steady flow through it.

Sergeant Gormley didn't hear the small popping of explosive going off, but he heard the shrieks from those closest to the airlocks when they did, and nothing could disguise the sound of the weakened airlocks when they made a loud, booming crack above the crowd as they strained to hold.

The sergeant cast an anxious eye over the rapidly dwindling crowd.

The airlocks cracked again, ominously loud, and he hung back behind the last of the crowd, uneasy. There were still too many people appearing out of nowhere; popping up onto the cargo deck as if emerging from quarters or jobs further down in the station.

Even after the bulk of the crowd had filtered through and the silence of their departure made the shrieking of the airlocks more painful to the ears, he lingered still.

A Fifth Worlder sprinted across the decking, darting past him and up the gangway to relative safety, and for the last time, Sergeant Gormley hesitated. The airlocks hissed and howled, and if this deck was lost to the vacuum of space without the gangway being sealed, all the people on the upper boarding deck would be lost, too; but there were still people running across the loading dock.

"Airlocks, sir!" yelled one of his men, from the upper hatch. "They're about to go! Everything's flashing purple up here!"

A crack of sound split Sergeant Gormley's ears as he whipped into the gangway and slammed shut the hatch. He stayed for a moment to set the manual lock as well, his ears popping, then barrelled up the gangway and through the upper hatch.

His men were there to heave him through, quick and panicked.

"The manual lock's stuck, sir! We can shut it, but we can't seal it!"

Sergeant Gormley heaved shut the manual close with a roar,

scattering Fifth Worlders nearby. He shook his head, bearlike, as if he'd received a blow to the ears, and salt water flew. Below, the last few who hadn't made it up to the boarding deck were sucked out the airlocks: he saw one through the maxiplex windows on deck, and another wail rippled through the Fifth Worlders as they saw the figure, too.

"Corporal!"

"Not to worry, sir," said that voice cheerfully in his ear. "I've got 'em. They've got a nice lot of toys onboard this sloop, and the stragglers aren't coming out too fast to catch. So long as their lungs can take it for a second or two, they'll be fine. Have you got the rest of them?"

"For now," the sergeant said grimly, swiping the back of his hand across his face to collect the remaining moisture there. He had no idea how he was supposed to get this gaggle of Fifth Worlders safely into the Time Corp sloop and away before the whole lot of explosives below went off.

Again, he lifted his voice as loudly as he could, but only those closest to him obeyed, and when they reached the swirling edges of chaos where everyone else simply milled and wailed, they stopped again.

Sergeant Gormley howled and bellowed, as did his men, but there was the barest forward motion in the chaos, and he had to stop for breath as he felt the debris in the lower deck impacting against the floor beneath him.

Certainly everything was going wrong. In fact, it had gone so far to the wrong that Sergeant Gormley wasn't sure it could possibly be put right: he had entirely bungled the whole affair and now, somewhere out in the universe there was a small, feral little girl who would pay a price so terrible that even she couldn't say it.

That feral little girl who had given him...a hat.

One emergency hat.

There was nothing else he could do. So, amidst the wailing of the sirens and the screams and the constant thump of flying debris beneath his feet, Sergeant Gormley took his emergency hat out of his pocket and rather fatalistically put it on.

At once, every Fifth Worlder in the chaotic melee stopped what they were doing and looked toward him. Even the moving parts in the crowd that were other races caught onto the sudden quiet, and looked to him. At last there was quiet. At last there was some kind of order that could be channelled.

And at last, Sergeant Gormley understood.

Unlike the hard-hats that signalled an emergency officer in the Fourth World orbiting station he'd come from, this soft hat signified that he was *someone*, and the Fifth Worlders here, ant-like, would follow every order now that they had an official leader. By extension, every other person in reach would follow the flow to get out safely.

"Right then," said the sergeant, clearing his throat and putting on his best authoritative voice. "*To* the right, *in* an orderly fashion now! Exit at your *right*, board the *sloop*, and *march*!"

Even to the end, he was terrified that they wouldn't get out in time. They marched methodically, orderly, and quickly, but there was so little time left, and the sloop would still need to get safely clear.

Sergeant Gormley redoubled his bellowing, but it wasn't enough.

Then, across the deck, through the shifting crowd, he saw a brief patch of stillness in the melee: someone folding himself a hat *very similar* to the one the sergeant himself wore, out of something vaguely the right colour.

Someone who then put that folded hat on his head and proceeded to direct the fleeing Fifth Worlders from his side of the deck, corralling outliers and sending them scurrying along with the others.

That someone was short, wearing a pair of coveralls that had seen better days—possibly even better decades—and directing the fleeing Fifth Worlders in a way that left no room to doubt his authority, despite the coveralls and the fact that his home-made hat was already beginning to unfold itself over his left ear.

Sergeant Gormley was pretty certain who that someone was, but he didn't dare to look too closely, just in case he found out for sure. He was aware that the less he had to do with Kez and Marx, the better it was for his peace of mind. He was quite certain it was better for both his health and his career, too. The Time Corp didn't take kindly to anyone other than themselves interfering with time, nor were they particularly careful about the width of the net with which they swept up malefactors.

In the last rush to get everybody onto the Time Corp sloop, the other Someone with a hat vanished, much to Sergeant Gormley's relief. Since he was apparently the highest ranking officer on board, he felt that it would have been his duty to arrest Marx for impersonating an officer, amongst other things, and he would very much prefer not to do his duty in this instance.

The corporal met him by the loading hatch, his face shiny with exertion and his hand already on the emergency shut button. Above the roar of milling Fifth Worlders, he yelled, "Are we good to go, sir?"

"Close her up!" bawled Sergeant Gormley. Over the comms, he roared, "Get us out of here!"

He still felt the crawling of fear and threat down his neck that didn't stop until, above the throb of the engines, he felt the impact of the blast that he couldn't see. The sloop surged in a burble of wails and screams, then settled again.

"I don't know how you do it, sir!" yelled the corporal, his shiny face made brighter in a combination of admiration and wonder. "Not a life lost! They'll never believe this back at the station!"

. . .

Sergeant Gormley retired to his cabin much later than he'd expected when he began his day. In fact, it wasn't even the same day when he did so. There had been an expected but exasperating amount of paperwork that went along with evacuating an orbiting fuel station and commandeering someone else's sloop, as well as losing a skip to an explosion, not to mention the regular paperwork that had to be done to enter the evidence they had collected into the station, along with the reasons why that evidence was not as prolific as had been expected.

In the end, it was early the next day that the sergeant finally escaped to his quarters, exhausted and still high on the excitement of the previous day. Once ensconced, it seemed impossible to do anything but stand there helplessly, wondering what he was waiting for and when the adrenaline running through his veins would allow him to sleep.

As he shuffled his feet, something hard and oblong hit Sergeant Gormley on the side of the head. Already dizzy with success, he flinched and staggered slightly, then picked up the chocolate bar that had thus assaulted him. He looked at it bemusedly for far too long, and that must have irritated the thrower, because a sharp voice said, "It didn't come down in a shower av rain, y'know!"

Where was that infernal kid *now?*

"Up 'ere," she said, and he looked up and to the left.

Kez's head poked out of the square patch of darkness where his air filter ought to have been fitted over the venting system; as he watched, she wriggled her shoulders out as well and hung where she could almost look him in the face.

"Lookit you!" she said. "Still alive an' everyfink!"

"You could have told me!" he said reproachfully.

"Did tell ya," she said. "Didden I? *Emergency 'at,* I said."

"You could," Sergeant Gormley said, trying to be reasonable; trying very hard not to pick her up and throw her out the porthole, "you could have been more specific about what I needed to do. The airlocks ruptured—people were being sucked out into space!"

She shook her head. "Not allowed, see? If I go tellin' you everyfink, it starts makin' patterns that lead back to me, and we're tryin' to *stop* the Fixed Points from gettin' unfixed. That's 'ow they gets unfixed, patterns leading back to certain people. That's 'ow Uncle Cheng found us, near as we can work out."

"Fixed Points? What do you mean, Fixed Points?"

"You know," she said. "Them bits in time wot 'as to happen for everyfing to sit right. If they don't happen, then other stuff wot's more flexible can't happen, either."

"I know what Fixed Points are!" the sergeant said, less than calmly.

"Why'd you *ask*—"

"I wanted to know why I was messing with a Fixed Point!"

"You wasn't messin' wiv it," she said, with that tough little grin that worried him even more now in retrospect. "You was stoppin' someone else from messin' wiv it, and sewin' time back into the right place, like."

"You mean I stopped—I stopped a Fixed Point from coming apart?"

"You oughtta sit down," Kez advised him. "You look a bit funny. Eat yer chocolate. You can't go 'round lookin' like that: they'll think you need to go on leave or summink."

"I do need to go on leave," the sergeant said, rather numbly. He had never in his life had the wish to interfere with Fixed Points or even time in general. He was quite happy when it flowed around him, gently buffeting him into the things he needed to meet with and layering him with wrinkles as it did so. "Every time I meet you, I feel like I lose about ten more years of my life. I was happy—"

"—bored, more like," she muttered.

"—here in my station, minding my own business." Out of sheer befuddlement, Sergeant Gormley did sit down, and he found himself opening the wrapper of the chocolate bar out of much the same feeling, which made Kez grin. He gave her a hard look back for it: he still felt badly done by. "You told me that nothing would happen if I saved them all."

"Nuffink did 'appen!"

"The whole station blew up!"

"Well, *yeah*. That's wot 'appens when someone goes and chucks a whole mess av explosives inna a fuel station, ain't it?"

It was, supposed Sergeant Gormley rather wildly, just a bit comforting that Kez at least still considered human death to be something, even if she regarded the loss of a whole fuel station as unworthy of consideration.

"Anyway," she added, "that's the bit wot was *s'posed* to 'appen. Just a bit av a bang, see? And then someone would get a bit av an idea that it wasn't too 'ealthy to stay where 'e was."

That settled it, he *had* seen Marx somewhere in that rapidly moving crowd.

"Did someone—" he stopped, his throat dry and somehow unable to produce a sound, and swallowed hard. When he felt that he could try again, he asked, "Did someone try to blow up the entire fuel station and all those people just to kill Marx?"

Kez frowningly considered it, then said, "Not *'zactly*. It was already gunna blow up, see? It *has* to blow up; lotsa little fings depends on it. But 'e wasn't gunna die, and someone wanted to make sure 'e *did* die."

"Someone who doesn't care about Fixed Points," the sergeant said, feeling sick.

"Fort you was feelin' better," she said accusingly. "Keep eatin' yer chocolate."

"You could," said Sergeant Gormley, still faintly protesting, "have helped a bit!"

"Ain't that some cheek!" Kez said. "'Ow'd you reckon you got access into their systems, eh? You don't reckon a Fourth World Orbiting Evidence Sergeant gets all pass access to everybody's fuel station do ya?"

"Oh," said Sergeant Gormley. Now that he thought about it, it didn't make any sense. "That was you?"

She grinned. "Not 'zactly me: reckon it was Arabella wot set that up for yer, but I ain't sure. Mikkel's still funny 'bout doin' stuff against the law, see?"

"Thank you!" the sergeant said, with very real gratitude. "That's how I knew what to do."

He thought about that again, and added, "Well, at least I *thought* I knew what I needed to do."

"Lookit you, savin' hundreds of lives!" Kez said admiringly. "Anyway, fanks for everything. Reckon I'll be seein' you again."

Sergeant Gormley tried not to shudder, and said with something only vaguely approaching sincerity, "I'm looking forward to it."

"That's the spirit!" said Kez, even more admiringly. "You better 'ave a lie-down, I reckon. Yer still lookin' a bit peaky. See ya next time."

Sergeant Gormley didn't see her go, but then, he very rarely did. One day, in the darkest depths of his nightmares, he would discover exactly what she did to get around in time and space.

For today, he was merely grateful to have escaped being blown up once again.

AT 14.00 LRT *TCS RESILIENT* FAILED TO CHECK IN WITH BASE station at their regular scheduled time. First in evidence is the subsequent contact by Base (Petty Officer Green and Commander Harper), the entirety of which is on record as follows.

Transcript:

Base/PO Green: TCS *Resilient*, you've failed to meet your scheduled check-in. Please reply.

no reply

Base/PO Green: *TCS Resilient*, please reply.

no reply

Base/PO Green: *TCS Resilient,* should an officer fail to reply a third time, Time Corp will take immediate offensive action. Please reply.

TCS Resilient/person unknown: That might be a bit hard, mate. They're in the brig.

Base/PO Green: Please repeat that.

TCS Resilient/person unknown: They're in the brig.

Base/PO Green: Please confirm, *TCS Resilient.* Is there a mutiny aboard? We warn you that a mutiny will be met with deadly force.

TCS Resilient/person unknown: Yeah, that's likely to make someone cop to mutiny, isn't it?

indistinguishable noises, what is suspected to be a scuffle, multiple uses of "sorry sir, he got away"

TCS Resilient/Sgt Gormley: Sorry about that, sir. This is Sergeant Gormley of the WAOF, Fourth World Orbiting Evidence Station, sir. What the er, previous person was trying to say was that the crew has locked themselves in the brig, and they're refusing to come out.

Base/PO Green: Sergeant Gormley, glad to hear from you. Please repeat what you just said.

TCS Resilient/Sgt Gormley: They've locked themselves in the brig, sir. Every man jack of 'em. I've had to commandeer the sloop in order to render assistance to refugees from a privately owned Fifth World Orbiting Fuel Station that blew up, and once aboard it was plain that the crew had known something of the attack. They refused to render assistance and at first signs of danger from the refugees, locked themselves in the brig to escape reprisals. Further investigation revealed they had provided safe harbour to a person pretending to be Time Corp personnel, who attempted to blow up the orbiting fuel station I mentioned earlier. If they hadn't locked themselves in the brig, I would have had to do it for their own safety, sir.

Pause of thirty seconds

Base/CDR Harper: This is Commander Harper, taking over. I very much hope you have the evidence to back up what you've just said, Sergeant, or I'll be having a word with your commanding officer over at the WAOF.

TCS Resilient/Sgt Gormley: Yes, sir. Some of our evidence is dead, but we've got quite a bit of visual evidence along with a trail my corporal dug up in the computerised systems.

Base/CDR Harper: We'll see it when you get here: you'll be given priority docking. Can you repeat your name and provide us with the name of your corporal for our records?

TCS Resilient/Sgt Gormley: Sergeant Gormley and Corporal Jones, sir. We'll contact you again when we enter your space.

Transmission End

AAR: Misuse and Apprehension of the TCS Resilient: page 1/20

FIXED POINTS OF REFERENCE

IT WAS TOMORROW, OR MAYBE YESTERDAY, AND KEZ HAD A *headache*. She was also grumpy, but that wasn't necessarily the fault of the headache; on any given day, Kez was inclined to be anything from mildly grumpy right up to feral. Today, she felt *cold* and *blue* and she had forgotten what those things felt like for a little while.

That made Kez frown. She had forgotten what it felt like. Why? What was so different about today?

Today, just as she had done every day for the last year, she had woken up in a different place with a gasp and a stab of fear that Marcus might finally have caught up with her again.

Alone and angry. Cold and fearful.

'Ang on, thought Kez. *Where's Marx? 'Ow come I'm not in the Upsydaisy?*

Who is Marx? asked a whisper inside her head.

"You shut up!" Kez said aloud, wrathfully. "Marx is—Marx is —I know 'oo 'e is, all right? 'E's the one wot takes care av us. And we got our own ship an' everyfink!"

But it seemed hard to remember Marx at the moment, and all Kez could seem to bring to mind was a memory of him asking her, "I ever tell you about the time I nearly died?"

Kez hadn't stopped kicking the side of his chair, which occupation had undoubtedly led to the question in the first place.

"You're always nearly flamin' dyin'," she had said. "*Wot* time?"

"That time on a Fifth World Orbiting Fuel Station, right in the middle of a Fixed Point: lots of fun, kiddo. You'll love it! It started..."

What was the rest of it, now? What had happened in the story?

He had told her that *yesterday*, thought Kez irritably. So why couldn't she remember the rest of it? And why wasn't Marx here? She was somehow quite sure he didn't exist right now, and that *wasn't all right*. She wasn't even sure the *Upsydaisy* existed, and she was quite certain that, here and now, she had been alone for more than a year, and there was no way Marx would have let that happen.

She found herself absent-mindedly scratching at a scar on her arm as if it were new, and that was puzzling, too. She'd had that for at least a year: Kez had gone back in time to try and stop Boris from dying, and Marcus had *nearly* caught her. But today it didn't feel like it should be on her body, and Boris felt very far away and untouchable, and today she could remember someone called Marx who shouldn't exist and should at the same time.

Her thoughts dragging on too slowly, Kez frowned ferociously and tried to keep focused on three important questions: where was Marx, why didn't he exist, and where was the *Upsydaisy*?

Those questions were too hard, so she turned her mind to questions that she could more easily answer instead. Where had she fetched up last night to sleep? And where, more importantly, could she get a bit of nosh to make sure she didn't get too small for her armoured stockings? They didn't work as well when they weren't skin-tight.

Kez looked around her, taking in the plain richness of her surroundings. She'd fetched up in a corner behind the out-jutting of a life-pod housing, hidden from the casual passerby but noticeable to anyone who came to check the housings and life-pods, if that was something that was done regularly.

Looked like it would be, she thought grumpily. The luxury of everything around her was easy to see: she was on what was probably the lowest deck, with all the staff and kitchen and such, but everything here was still top quality and gold-trimmed.

Kez looked closer at the gold-trimmed logo that had been etched into the life-pod, and grinned a bit. Well, at least everything wasn't bad. She was aboard the *Chaebol*. She let herself grin about her good fortune for a minute or two before she tried to remember why it was such good fortune and failed. It was ridiculous to think that she knew someone rich enough to be on board one of the great space liners—especially one that was privately owned.

'Ang on, she thought suspiciously. *I know it's privately owned. Wot else do I know? An' how come I know it?*

She wanted, very desperately, to kick someone in the shins.

And then, all of a sudden, as if the furious desire to strike back had jostled something loose, Kez remembered.

She was in another version of now. Uncle Cheng was messing with Fixed Points, and she and Marx and TuanTuan had decided they needed to do something about it; but no one had been quite sure *what* except for TuanTuan. He had done something—she couldn't remember what, exactly, right now—but Kez knew she had expected to go into that other reality with Marx to help her, occupying the bodies of the alternate versions of themselves. So where *was* Marx? More importantly, why wasn't he with her?

He was supposed, thought Kez, her eyes prickling with hot tears of rage, to always *be there*. The world looked blue and cold around her and she didn't know why, and she didn't know how to change it.

The *Chaebol*, she now remembered, with a sudden surge of almost overwhelming relief, was a good place to find herself, for the simple reason that she might be able to find a version of TuanTuan here—if she'd come to the right time as well as place. And TuanTuan would be able to figure out what had gone wrong, and why she had arrived in another reality by herself when they had prepared for her and Marx to go together.

If Marx wasn't here, she was going to get this reality's Tuan-Tuan to help her go back and kick *her* TuanTuan in the shins for getting it wrong.

Kez sat where she was, angrily plotting, until a staff member came up to check on the life-pod and looked a bit too kindly at her. Then she rose, hauled her stockings up, and trotted away in search of food. The kindly-looking staff member might have given her some, but then Kez would have felt that she had to either be grateful or bite the woman, and most places caused a bit of a fuss when you bit staff. No, she would much rather steal the food; it would save her from the annoyance of knowing that she was supposed to be grateful but somehow only able to bite.

Kez found her way to the staff mess hall quite easily; it was also very easy to slip into a recently vacated booth and eat the remains of the meals of the two people who had just quitted the booth. There were enough kids around that she didn't look out of place, either.

That done, Kez swiped the back of her arm across her mouth to evenly distribute the remainder of food there, and tried to think what she should do.

Marx should be here, with her, she thought, picking at the scar on her arm. But he wasn't, and she couldn't look for him because—because—

Kez tried to push that thought away. Her best option was still to look for TuanTuan if she couldn't find Marx. And after that—or maybe before, depending on where she had arrived in the timeline—she was going to find out what had happened to Marx in this reality so that they could stop it. Because if Marx wasn't here with her, it was because there hadn't been a body in this reality for him to come *to*. He was dead.

At least she'd come out aboard the *Chaebol*: in her own reality, it was home to the Li family even if it no longer housed their heir, Tuan Li, who had legitimately escaped from his family and earned his freedom. Kez was pretty sure they still kept tabs on TuanTuan. He tended to duck about in the WAOF these days, though she knew he occasionally saw his family, so if he wasn't home for a visit, it might be hard to find him.

Kez remembered roughly where the family quarters were, in the bit of her brain that had her own memories and not the memories of this Marxless Kez. She made a quick slip upward and inward, careful to avoid the centre of the ship on the vague memory of something huge and toothy and clever, and came out a bit too early.

Noise and lights burst into being around her as she stepped out into a party, fending off fronds from some exotic plant that tickled across her face. She'd come out behind the potted plants.

Kez chuckled beneath her breath. She might not have come out in just the place she wanted, but at least she'd come out where no one could see her.

Well, not quite no one: someone was leaning against the bar a few steps away from her, dressed in blue silk and blue suede shoes, and his eyes were on her when she noticed him. He stood alone, which worried Kez a bit when she could see that the room was really very crowded.

What worried her more was the fact that she recognised him and didn't recognise him at the same time. Here was TuanTuan, but he wasn't exactly TuanTuan as she remembered him. The TuanTuan Kez knew was all softness and fluffiness, his mono-lid eyes shadowed but shyly shining below the full, heavy fringe of his hair; the thumb and forefinger of one hand always tugging at the bit of hair behind his ear. This TuanTuan was glittering and bright, his eyes brilliant and very hard, and beneath the collar of his shirt and the frothiness of his cravat, she saw the gleam of a familiar collar, too.

Kez stared right back at him, then took a few steps toward him, her eyes running over the collar once again.

"Flamin' 'eck!" she said, colder and bluer than before. "Wot you still got that thing for? Got rid of that ages ago!"

He looked at her curiously. "Where did you come from?"

"Same as usual," Kez told him, batting away the last of the fronds from the nearby plants. She grinned at him by way of welcome, trying to banish the cold feeling. Even if he did still have his collar on in this reality, he should recognise her. "Wot you all dollied up for, TuanTuan?"

"My mother prefers me to look my best," said Tuan. "What did you mean, why have I *still got that thing*?"

"Heck," said Kez, the grin of welcome withering away utterly. She hadn't wanted to let the memories of this Kez bubble up, but she ought to have done so. The memories of this Kez had nothing in them that related to Tuan outside their first meeting in the Institute; no further meeting when she had released him from his collar—no meeting later still, when they had found that the death of his real parents was a Fixed Point and that they couldn't get close enough to rescue them.

Furiously, she said, "Wot 'appened? 'Oo went and messed that bit up as well, I'd like to know!"

"I have questions, too," said Tuan, pushing away from the bar and stooping just slightly to adjust his height closer to hers. "For example, I'd very much like to know why your presence here is making *this* do *this*."

Kez peered at the tiny box he thrust in her direction, and saw numbers flashing up and up and *up*. "Wot the flamin' 'eck's *that*?"

"That's what I'd like to know," he said, pushing the little box back in his pocket. "For your information, this is a little device that measures increments of change to the fabric of reality."

"See you still don't speak like a normal person," Kez observed. "Guess that ain't changed, anyway."

Tuan opened his mouth to make what she was quite sure would have been a hot reply, but shut it again. After appearing to struggle with himself for another few moments, he said, "I've been tracking warped reality since last Tuesday LRT, but I'm quite certain it goes back further than that."

"'Ow's that, then?"

"It's like trying to explain to a cat with sunstroke," muttered Tuan. "Something happened last Tuesday that did something odd to reality. I only noticed it because I was looking for something else and I know a little about memories that aren't real. I made *this* little thing so I could keep an eye on it and establish a pattern. Then you come along and it's going crazy."

"Yeah, I s'pose that could 'appen," she said. "'E reckoned

people might be able to tell where we'd been over 'ere, even if we weren't *here*, like."

"Which brings me right back to the question of who you are," said Tuan, with another cold smile.

"At least I'm meself," Kez told him accusatorily. "Ain't all dollied up wiv different expressions an' stuff."

She hadn't expected this. None of them had.

"Nobody knows why those points are fixed," Marx had told her, after they received the portentous Newlands Box the last time. "But we know they have to stay fixed, or the universe falls apart."

"One or two might be all right," her TuanTuan had said. "The universe as we know it wouldn't still exist, but it wouldn't fall apart straight away, either: it'd just be a different one. Maybe a few different ones. But we also don't know how many points have to be unfixed before everything does fall apart."

"Exactly," had said Marx, smiling grimly. "We don't know. And we don't want to know. So we'd better do something about it."

Yeah, thought Kez now, fiercely. *Well, I'm gunna. An' if you blokes aren't here to help me, I'm gunna do it by myself this time. I'll save yas and then you'd better flamin' let me fly the Upsydaisy!*

But there was no Marx in this version of the universe to hear her, and that made Kez even angrier.

"Get yer mug outta my face," she muttered at Tuan, and stomped away to the buffet table. What she wanted to do was blow up the soup in the faces of all these well-dressed, rich, sharp-toothed people, but if she did that, there was no Marx to take advantage of the distraction and do...something. Something, what? What would Marx have done?

Marx would have figured out the problem, and then decided on a solution.

What was the problem?

The problem was that Kez needed to get home.

No, the problem was that she needed to find out exactly

where Uncle Cheng had dislodged the Fixed Point in this part of space and time so that TuanTuan could link it to a time in their own reality where they could do something about it.

Then she had to get home.

Solution, thought Kez. Now she needed a solution.

"I wish you wouldn't look at things like that," said the Tuan whose expressions she didn't recognise. He had followed her from the bar, slowly and leisurely. "It worries me."

"Yeah, well, some things never change, eh," Kez said absently. She would have punched the TuanTuan she knew—told him to mind his own business and not to tell her what to do with her own face.

Kez found that she almost didn't dare to do it to this Tuan, and that annoyed her so much that she kicked him instead.

"Don't tell me what to do wiv me face," she told him as he gasped, clinging to the thin shank she'd assaulted. "Tryin' to figger out me solution."

"Oh, is that all?" panted Tuan, straightening with less dignity than before. "I should have you thrown out, you awful little feral!"

"Ain't no fun in that, TuanTuan," Kez told him. "I'd only get back in, anyways."

What she needed was—actually, what she really needed was TuanTuan. She wasn't clever with figuring out things like Tuan-Tuan was; he was the one who'd pinpointed the Fixed Points that were most likely to be in danger in the first place.

This Tuan wasn't as good as her TuanTuan, but he was the only thing she had.

And Kez's thought process grew crystal clear.

Problem: What had caused the Fixed Point to become unfixed? And how would Kez get home?

Solution: Get Tuan to figure out both problems.

Something of her TuanTuan must be in there somewhere, even if he didn't recognise her: he would help her if she asked him—if she explained to him exactly what had gone wrong. That was another problem, because Kez only very loosely understood exactly what had gone wrong with the universe. She was quite certain that TuanTuan would know, anyway.

"Oi," she said, by way of getting the conversation back along the lines of what was useful. "That liddle box. Wot's all that about, then?"

"Something very odd has been going on in the universe lately," said Tuan thoughtfully, flexing the leg she had kicked. He almost sounded like her TuanTuan, which was disorienting and annoying.

Kez had to try very hard not to scowl at him, but some of the pebbly hardness must have returned to her eyes, because he looked away.

"Connections in the universe that were once in one position are now in another. And the funny thing about those—"

He stopped and seemed to fall into deep thought, which Kez knew in her own TuanTuan was a matter of him forgetting the world around him as he considered the problem at hand deep in the recesses of his own mind. He would come out of it sooner or later, with something very important to say.

Sometimes, it was necessary to prod him out of such moods by the application of a very clammy, very surprised toilet-clinger frog to the back of the neck; it never seemed to affect the usefulness of his conclusions, and it did streamline things.

Kez considered her options, weighing up the usefulness of cold jelly as opposed to the less cold flummery with its likelihood of swiftly growing discomfort, but Tuan came out of his thoughts as suddenly as he'd become lost in them.

"Whatever it is, it's firmly fixed to you," he said. "As far as I can work out, last Tuesday has been fused with today, and I'm certain you arrived today."

"Your liddle box tell ya that?"

"Indirectly," he said. "Until last Tuesday, there was another thread pulling along with yours—as soon as that disappeared, there was a great big twitch of time and space and something vanished."

"Wot vanished?" she demanded.

"I don't know," he said. "That's the thing about existing in a reality—if someone goes changing things that should happen so that they don't happen, you don't know what that thing was. It doesn't exist here anymore. I can only see the currents of where and when it was."

"Last Tuesdee," said Kez, nodding.

"Yes," Tuan agreed. "And you."

"Me, wot?"

"And it was connected with you."

"Wasn't 'ere last Tuesdee," she said instinctively, although she knew better. "Weren't me."

Someone ain't just messin' wiv Fixed Points, she thought. *They're messin' wiv Fixed Points what affect us. The flamin' cheek!*

Or, she wondered suddenly, meditating for perhaps the first time on the cluttered mess of destruction and chaos she had left in her wake for as long as she could remember, was it that the particular gift she had been born with had so much affected the universe around her that those Fixed Points, those necessary actions that must happen to keep the universe in its current state, had been formed from the detritus of her chaotic passage? And having been formed from her passage, the destruction of them was tearing away from her every loved thing and necessary adjunct?

Things like Marx, who should have come along but hadn't.

A thread that had once been tangled with hers but wasn't in this reality.

Something that happened last Tuesday, or *didn't* happen last Tuesday, and changed the whole course of reality in this version of the universe.

She remembered TuanTuan from her own reality, "We've passed through a statistically large amount of Fixed Points at the moment of their fixing—all three of us. Sometimes two or all of us at once. There are more Fixed Points than the ones we've been through, but—"

"But we've seen more than our fair share," Marx had said grimly.

But here and now, Marx was dead. And him being dead had made such a big problem for a Fixed Point that it had begun to come apart, which was bad for reality as well as for Kez.

Suddenly, the memory that had been floating around in her head came back again. Marx saying, "I ever tell you about that time I nearly died?" and "Right in the middle of a Fixed Point. Tuesday morning, bright and early—too bright and early, if you ask me..."

Kez thought about that very carefully, then asked Tuan, "Wot 'appens—wot 'appens if someone wasn't meant to die and there's a Fixed Point kinda dependin' on 'im not dyin'? And then someone goes and makes perishin' *sure* 'e dies?"

"I would assume that the Fixed Point would become unfixed," said Tuan, very thoughtfully. "Shedding warped reality everywhere. Leaving a scar where it once was, surrounded by more warped reality. I knew—oh I knew this was going to be an interesting week!"

"'Ow d'you fix summink like that, then? Wiv that liddle box?"

"You don't," Tuan said. The other TuanTuan had tried to explain it to her, too, she rather thought. Some of the memories still weren't quite all there yet. "You *can't*—not personally, anyway, I should think. A person responsible for forming a Fixed Point going back to that exact point would be in great danger of unmaking the Point themselves. So would anyone too closely connected with them."

Kez, with a vague memory of having asked much the same question of her own TuanTuan in her home reality, asked, "Yeah, but wot if you was *really* careful an' stuff?"

"It doesn't matter how careful you are," Tuan said, surprisingly patient. She had an idea that she had managed to capture his imagination with her questions. "You wouldn't be able to touch it again without doing what you're trying to prevent."

Kez, who when she was told to get her hands off something was inclined to reach out to touch it with her feet out of pure spite, made a very important connection between that pernicious part of her personality and her current situation.

Tuan said, "What a dreadful grin! Whatever are you going to do *now*? You better not be thinking about kicking me again."

"Nah," she said, grinning even more savagely. "Got n'idea."

"Murder, by the look of it," said the Tuan who was not TuanTuan.

"Wish you'd stop lookin' at me from 'is face," Kez said irritably. She stabbed a finger at his collar. "Oi. Want me to get rid av' that for ya?"

Tuan went very white, and for quite some time she thought he wouldn't answer at all.

Then, at last, he said pleasantly, "It's a bit late for that, don't you think?"

Kez stared at him, aware in some uncomfortable way that she'd made a misstep and unable to decide exactly how. At last, she said, "You're too old. An' you got sharp. Why'd you get sharp, TuanTuan?"

"Why do you keep calling me that, by the way?" he asked, leaning his hip against the buffet table as if he had unwound from the deadly stillness of before.

"It's yer name."

"It's not, you know," he said. "My name is Tuan Li—I'm sorry, did you say something?"

"Nuffink," she muttered. What she had said, before she thought about it, was that his name wasn't even Tuan Li—they had just kept calling him by Tuan because it was too hard to tell where in the timeline they were whenever they met him, and TuanTuan was always a bit confused about who he was before a certain time.

"And most people," he added, his voice cold, "call me *Master* Li."

Kez shot a look up at him over the top of the sweet pretzel she'd swiped from the buffet. "Yeah? Wot they do that for?"

"My commanding presence, I suppose," he said, and his voice was so bitter that Kez almost regretted being cheeky. A moment later, she was glad she had been, because he added, with more amusement than she'd yet heard from him, "I see that it doesn't seem to have affected you. Have your parents been starving you feral, or are you trying to make your way through the entire buffet out of spite, by the way?"

"Ain't got parents," Kez said, reaching for a chocolate doughnut with sweet, powdery fingers. "You ain't, either, but I s'pose you already figured that out."

"I have figured out a lot of things," said Tuan, his face stiff with shock. "But I would very much like to know how you figured out some of the things you're coming out with."

"You an' me are friends," she told him. She still felt crabbed and unsure, so she snatched up another doughnut to hold in her other hand, glaring at Tuan to dare him to say anything about it. "When you ain't got that collar on. Want me to take it off?"

"You asked that before," he said, and this time he seemed to be able to speak properly. "And I wish I knew if you meant it!"

"Only one way to find out," Kez said, her voice muffled by alternate bites of glazed and chocolate doughnut. "All you gotta do is say yes."

"How—what do you know about my parents?" he asked. "My father's dead, but my mother is still very much alive. That's her across the room in gold spangles."

Kez snorted a few flakes of glaze onto his shiny coat-front. "That's wot they told yer, anyway."

"I know she's not my mother," Tuan said, giving up the pretence and directing a cold, narrow look down at her. "But what I would like to know is how *you* know it."

"Shoulda asked that, shouldn't ya?" grumbled Kez. She tried

to reach for another sweet, but Tuan seized her wrist and removed her hand from the vicinity of the table.

"I'm asking now."

"Right!" said Kez. "I know it 'cos you an' me are friends in anovver reality, see? We tried to save your family, but we couldn't get close enough 'cos it was one av them Fixed Points. Time Corp has 'em wrapped up real tight—well, it used to 'ave 'em all wrapped up tight. Uncle Cheng's been messin' wiv 'em 'cos 'e don't know how to take *no* for an answer, so these days they're a bit looser, if ya get me meanin'."

"I don't at all," Tuan said. "But if I'm guessing rightly, you're claiming that you've come to see me via a wrinkle in reality that's been caused by a Fixed Point becoming a bit less fixed."

Kez looked at him accusingly. "You *did* know!"

"I *did* try to tell you that I'd been coming across warped reality!" protested Tuan, and for a brief moment, he was exactly the TuanTuan she knew. "You refused to understand!"

"That's 'cos you can't talk proper!" instantly retorted Kez. "Anyway, that's 'ow I know wot I know, and that's wot I'm tryin' to fix."

"The me back there," Tuan said, his fingers running across the collar around his neck, as though unconsciously, "does he— do I wear this collar?"

"Nah," Kez told him. "Got rid of it for ya."

"Why did you come to find me tonight? Specifically me, I mean? I assume it wasn't just to help yourself to my buffet."

"Need yer help wiv all this," Kez explained. "Figured it was worth lookin' for ya here first."

"Playing with Fixed Points is ridiculously dangerous."

"'Course it's dangerous," she said. "It's always dangerous. Ain't ever stopped us before—ain't like we've ever 'ad a choice before, 'f'it comes to that."

"I'm not in the habit of putting myself in danger for people I've just met," Tuan said coolly. "I don't even do it for family allies, unless they pay very well. And I'm far more valuable to the family than the payment we can get from anything too dangerous."

"Ain't got money," Kez told him, perplexed. "I came 'ere 'cos you're me friend, *and* you got brains."

"Maybe I was that friend once," Tuan said, with a distant, hard look to his eyes. "I haven't been that person for very many years, I can assure you. Whether or not you know me in another reality, I see no reason to put myself at risk to help you."

"That's funny," said Kez, even though it wasn't really. "'Cos you still got that thing 'round yer neck. Don't reckon you'd still 'ave that if you believe the guff you're tellin' me: reckon you've been givin' Auntie Li some trouble."

He didn't pretend to misunderstand. "Auntie L—my mother prefers me to be within...calling distance. Or shall we say, calling *ability*. She doesn't like having to wait, and she certainly doesn't care to have to fetch me from sloops and far-flung planets when I slip my handlers."

"Reckon you're a bit old to be wearin' it, ain't ya?"

"My opinion isn't asked," he said, softly and coldly.

"You want me to take it off, or not? I came 'ere to ask you to help me, so I might as well."

"Ah," said Tuan, settling back with folded arms. It seemed to Kez that his face grew harder. "There it is. I wondered what you'd want in exchange."

"Ain't an exchange," Kez said. "You just gotta ask. I'll take it off whether or not you 'elp me."

"What a lovely fiction," said Tuan, smiling a sharp, brittle smile.

"Told ya," she said. "All you gotta do is say yes. I'll sort it out."

"I can't do that," he said tightly. "Because nothing comes without a cost, even friendship. Especially friendship."

Kez stared at him. There was something broken and frightening about this Tuan: something more akin to Kez herself than the sweet, hopeful boy she knew. The steel core beneath the fluffiness was the same, but it had been twisted, and that *wasn't all right.*

The problem had become somewhat different—had split into a second problem, in fact.

Problem #2: This Tuan wasn't *her* TuanTuan, and did not seem at all willing to help. The kick to the shins might be considered problem #2.5, in fact.

Solution #2?

Kez grinned.

"Don't grin at me like that!"

Solution #2: Kidnap Tuan.

The collar was the first consideration when it came to putting that plan into action. Kez had done something about it once before, but she wasn't quite sure it would be the same this time. She wasn't even sure it was the same collar. It was certainly the first thing she would have to do if she wanted to kidnap Tuan, however: through the collar, Auntie Li had not only the ability to track Tuan, but to haul him back to her side through time and perhaps space.

Auntie Li wasn't the only one who could track them by it: there was also a beastie of uncertain origins and unexplained talents that lived in the centre of the *Chaebol* that could and would track them should someone go too far away while wearing the collar, or remove it too clumsily. A beastie that would slaughter anyone within the vicinity of the collar, but not wearing it. It had almost killed all three of them in the other reality.

"If you're just going to grin at me like that," said Tuan, edging away ever so slightly, "I'm going to leave you to security."

"Reckon that jelly bowl's big enough to absorb a bit av an explosion?" Kez asked him, brushing the powdered sugar from her hands and onto her flowered dress as she stepped forward. "Just enough so I don't go killin' people, I mean? Don't matter if we make a bit av a mess, mind."

It seemed like he couldn't help the professional glance he

threw at the jelly bowl, but that expression was very quickly replaced with one of wary fear. "Don't you *dare*—" he began, but Kez already had a good grip on his wrist, and that was all she needed.

"'Ere we go!" she said exultantly.

Kez moved herself and Tuan and the collar into the milky whiteness of the Other Zone, where there wasn't time or space for the collar to explode as it had been designed to do if it was removed. Tuan had already fainted: people in general, Kez had found, didn't react very well to the Other Zone.

She reached up and grasped the collar, separating its being from Tuan's being, then put it back in time and space very carefully where it could explode gloriously in a sloppy shower of blue jelly.

Kez regretted not being able to see that: there were so many people in white nearby that it was certain to have been spectacular. But there were more important things to take care of right now: that was what Marx would have said. So Kez, feeling very grown up and responsible, brought the inert Tuan back into that reality's timestream with a carefully calculated preciseness to exactly when and where they needed to be.

That brought them into a white, breezy room with no windows but a good, fresh ventilation system and soft carpet. A number of gaming systems and other leisure activities were scattered around the room, and a training simulator took up an entire corner in the form of a tube of reinforced maxiplex from floor to ceiling.

Tuan collapsed onto the carpet before Kez could do more than grab the front of his shiny collar-points to slow his descent so that he didn't hit his head.

"Heck!" she said. "You're too flamin' heavy, TuanTuan!"

"My name," whispered Tuan, blinking groggily, "is Tuan. Don't baby me."

"Careful," Kez told him. "'F'you sit up too quick you're gunna —Blimey, that's a bit colourful! Wot you been eatin', TuanTuan?"

Tuan retched one last time, shivering, and managed by some miracle to avoid soiling his clothes as well as the carpet. When he had stopped shivering, he edged away from the messy patch of carpet and climbed to his feet with a dignity and poise that made Kez grin.

"Well," he said coolly, "you've got me. I should think you've got about five minutes to enjoy the triumph of it before my mother's ship-beastie gets here to remind you that victory is only fleeting. It won't harm me, but I do assure you it will take you apart in seconds."

"Flamin' cheerful, ain't ya? *Well*, clever clogs! You might wanna 'ave a feel of yer neck."

He clapped one hand to his neck, then the other, eyes wide with shock. "How did you do that! *How*? It was rigged to—"

"Explode," Kez finished for him. "Yeah. Told ya: I've already sorted it out once. You ain't even asked 'ow we got here."

"I remember that perfectly well," Tuan said, clearing his throat. "I don't usually lose my lunch that easily, I can promise you!"

"You was out fer it!" she protested.

"Not as much as all that," he said. "Don't ever take me there again!"

"Funny that," Kez said. "Marx don't like it when I takes 'im there, either."

"That's *beside the point*!" Tuan said in exasperation. "The only difference you've made by taking off the collar is to sentence me to death as well!"

Kez made a *pft!* sound that appeared to irritate him. "'Aven't, though," she said.

"You don't understand how the collar and the beastie *work*."

"Bet I do."

He narrowed his eyes at her, his jaw tight. "Whatever it is you do to move through space—"

"—an' time."

"I beg your pardon?"

"I moves through space *an'* time," she told him.

He gazed at her, aghast. "That's what that was? The Other Zone? But that's worse! If you've taught the beastie how to get there, there's no hope for me! I might as well let it kill me right now: it'll follow me through space *and* time when I do manage to escape!"

"Nah, so long as it don't *see* me doin' it, it can't learn it," she said, grinning. That memory was sparkling, crystal clear, etched in remembered fear. "Ask me 'ow I knows!"

"I would assume that's part of the *you and I are friends* thing you keep telling me," Tuan said.

"Yeah," she said. "That, and this time I took it off ya in the Other Zone, not while we was in time. We're back a bit, before I kidnaps yer: the beastie don't know you're gone, yet."

He stared at her with his mouth open for quite some time before he cleared his throat and said, "I told you—I said I wouldn't help you. Just because you took the collar off, it doesn't mean I owe you anything. You're obviously clever enough to sort out something by yourself."

There was a bitterness deep in Kez's heart. She had really thought that if she showed Tuan she was willing to help him, it would prompt an emergence of the TuanTuan she had known.

She could threaten to take him back into the Other Zone and leave him there.

She could threaten to leave a leg or an arm behind, next time.

She could threaten to take him right back to Auntie Li, who wouldn't, Kez was quite sure, be forgiving.

Instead, bitterly, she said, "Off ya go, then."

"I beg your pardon?"

"You can go!" Kez shouted. "Ain't gunna force ya to do anyfink!"

She'd thought she could do it, and maybe she might have been able to do it before she met Marx, but Kez had neither the stomach nor the desperation for it anymore. She had lived with that desperation once, and it was disconcerting to find that there were things she would no longer do, though she would once readily have done them dire circumstances.

"I can assure you that I won't change my mind," Tuan warned. "I won't be made to help you in this hair-brained scheme just because you saw fit to kidnap and free me."

"I know," muttered Kez. "Just get lost, orright? I know you ain't 'im. The door's right over there: reckon you can get pretty far away before the time comes 'round again."

"It's not good glaring at me, either."

"I ain't glarin'!"

"I won't," said Tuan, his chest rising and falling just a bit too fast, "be emotionally blackmailed into helping you. I didn't ask you to free me. I told you I wouldn't accept it."

"Yeah, yeah. Why'ju fink I kidnapped ya?"

"I didn't ask you to free me!"

"Yeah, got it! The door's over there, bucko! It ain't locked!"

"You're not going to make me change my mind by pretending to be nice, so you might as well stop it. I'm not the kind of person who can be manipulated like that. I only help people when I can get something out of it, too!"

"If yer going," Kez said, with another flash of temper, "just flamin' go! Stop tellin' me 'ow narsty you are an' stuff."

This time, he really did turn and walk away, and Kez sat where she was on the carpet, tired and weepy and angry. She took in a huge breath of air and let it out in an angry, explosive gush that was almost a sob but couldn't afford to be.

She still had to find out how to get back to her own reality: now that she didn't have Tuan to help her she would need to come up with something on her own. At the very least, she could try to save Marx while she was here. If she went back in time—

And then it occurred to Kez that Tuan was still standing by the door, one foot nearly out and the other still angled toward her.

"Fort you was goin'," she said, glaring at him.

"I *was*," he said, lifting his chin. "But I've thought of something I want."

"Yeah? Fort you said—"

"If you don't stop telling me what you thought I said, I really will go away," snapped Tuan.

Kez narrowed her eyes at him, but decided against further incendiary speech. "Wot you want, then?"

"I told you," said Tuan, turning back into the room. "I *told* you that everything costs something. If I help you, you have to take me with you. I can't stay here—they'll just capture me again, and it'll be worse than before."

"Can't," Kez told him. "Already got a TuanTuan back in my reality. If you come over—if you try to smoosh in there wiv 'im—"

She was already aware of exactly how fragmented an existence it was, living inside the brain of another version of herself; to be neither herself nor the version of herself whose body she inhabited. The memories of both oddly overlapping and not quite clear on everything.

"It'll still be your friend as well as me," Tuan said. "You've still got both sets of memories, haven't you?"

"Yeah," Kez said. "But the other one's memories are sorta... fadin', and ain't nothin' real clear. You ain't gunna come wiv me to take over 'is brain and body. You ain't him."

"I could be—I once was."

"You ain't him," she said again, flintily. "Dunno wot 'appened to you, but my TuanTuan wouldn't never try to take over someone else's body an' steal the rest av their life. Someone already done that to 'im and I won't let it 'appen again."

"You—" he stopped, frustrated, and said, "I'll stay, but this isn't the last I'll say about it."

"Yeah," said Kez. "You keep talkin' 'til you're blue in the face. Ain't gunna change nuffink."

Tuan's head ducked in a laugh that he tried to hide. He cleared his throat and asked, "Where are we, by the way?"

Kez grinned at him. "Wouldn't *you* like to know?"

He looked around him, frowning. "No matter how far away I am, they'll still find me eventually."

"Yeah," she said. "But it'll take 'em a while, and that's all we need, see? Just long enough for you to do that liddle brain thing you do and figure out 'ow to send me back—and 'ow to save me friend."

"What friend?" asked Tuan, still gazing around the room. His head tilted to one side, and his eyes grew very wide. "Wait. Is this—is this one of the staff recreation rooms on the *Chaebol*?"

"Got it in one!" Kez crowed. "They know you left 'cos I made sure to leave a bit av a trail, see? It'll take 'em at least a day to figger out you're still on the sip and that it's not just the sensors playin' up and makin' two of ya. I popped us here a bit earlier."

"You're actually terrifying," Tuan said, in wonder. He asked again, "What friend? Not the other me, I take it?"

"Marx," Kez said. She explained, "'E's the one wot looks after me. Only he can't here 'cos Uncle Cheng did summink wot made sure 'e died instead av livin'."

"You think his death is the aberration that broke the Fixed Point?"

"Yeah," she said shortly. "*Tuesday*, you said. An' I bet I can tell you where the things started—started *wrinklin'* when it comes to this bit av the universe, too."

Tuan stared at her. "I believe you can. Where was it, then? If you're wrong, I'm going to leave you here and go back to the party just before you kidnap me."

"Last Tuesdee, on a Fifth World orbitin' fuel station, innit?"

"You—*how* did you know that? My instruments are the only ones of their kind in the known Twelve Worlds, and—"

"Firteen," muttered Kez.

"What?"

"You forgot Thirteenth World," she enunciated clearly.

"There's nothing there but trees and beasties," said Tuan.

"There's not much to remember. And it's not classified as a world, *technically*."

"Yeah, and I ain't classified as a person," Kez told him. *"Technically*. Technically, I'm s'posed to be dead."

"I'm honestly very surprised that you're not," Tuan said. "And yet, somehow I'm not. All right, I said I would stay, so I will. How do you know that's the place?"

"Told yer," she said. "Some av these Fixed Points is attached to us—this one was where Marx wos meant to escape, an' I reckon someone made sure 'e died instead."

He took in a deep breath. *"How* is it possible—no, never mind that. You can move unaided through time and space. You're obviously connected to the roots of the universe and anyone connected with you would be likely to get attached, too. Very well; your friend is the mooring for this particular Fixed Point, and it's likely that the unloosing of it has created this particular version of reality."

"Got it in one," Kez said, gloomily congratulatory.

"No doubt they picked the one that would benefit them the best," mused Tuan. "They would have dismantled the one that gave them the best benefit for the danger it brought about. Do you know what it is they want? The people who split this Fixed Point from its moorings?"

Kez shot her fiercest grin at him. "Reckon that'd be me: real popular, I am. But they 'ave an 'ard time gettin' at me wiv Marx gummin' up the works."

He muttered something that could have been, "I'll bet."

"An' prob'ly they don't wanna die. That sorta thing."

"Both good reasons. Are you trying to kill anyone, by the way?"

"Nope," Kez said, succinctly. "But sometimes stuff 'appens, and Marx ain't always careful if 'e thinks someone's tryin' to 'urt me."

"I see," said Tuan, eyeing her warily. "Very well, if we want to figure out which Fixed Points they're most likely to have meddled with, I'll need to update my software. I'd only found one aberration, but if I can refine it enough with what you've told me—"

He trailed away into a thoughtful silence; but while he was silent and apparently unresponsive, his fingers were busy about the controls of the console. Kez, well aware by now of the vagaries of her own TuanTuan, allowed him to continue so for quite some time without either interruption or inconvenience.

When it appeared that his face was beginning to work again, and his eyes began flickering across the screen as his fingers moved, she asked, "Wot you doin'?"

"I'm running my scenarios again," he explained. "But I'll only finalise the software this coming week, so I've had to update it manually with what I already know. I want to know if anything's changed exactly today to bring about the changes I discovered earlier."

That didn't make much sense to Kez, but Tuan's explanations often didn't. She let him do what he did, and wandered closer to the training pod that was attached to the console. It said *do not touch*, so she poked it and received a tiny electric shock for her trouble that made her scowl at it.

When she turned around again, already bored, Tuan was typing at the console with great speed and efficiency; he didn't seem to be doing so with success, however, because as she watched, he stopped, perplexed, and frowned.

While she watched, he fiddled with the controls and frowned again. Aloud, he said, "From my calculations, there are another two realities that have now split off. It wasn't like this last time I looked—I'm fairly certain, at any rate. This reality split was from today, but the other realities—"

"'Ang on!" interrupted Kez. "You mean there are *more* av these other realities *right now*?"

"As many as there are Fixed Points that are altered. If it was me, I would have picked the three most likely to bring about the effects I wanted, and dismantled them one by one to see which one got me what I wanted. If I got what I wanted after the first, I wouldn't need to use the others."

"Flamin' 'eck!" Kez said, going cold. "It's happenin' here, too! Reckon there's about five Fixed Points wot are attached to us; he's got enough to play wiv."

He stared at her. "You—that—the universe will fall apart!"

"Only if they undoes all of 'em," she said, trying to be comforting. She couldn't help the grin that came out, though. Since hope of comfort was gone, she added, "They're gunna, too. That's why I'm here—it's wot we're tryin' to stop in my reality, TuanTuan."

"There are only twenty Fixed Points in the entirety of time and space!" Tuan said, in shock. "Are you trying to tell me that *five* of those are connected to you?"

She grinned at him. "Oi."

"W—what?"

"One av 'em is attached to you, too."

"Don't—I didn't want to know that!"

"Yeah? But it's 'elpful, ain't it? That's back when we met for the first time: reckon they did summink to that one, too."

That made him more thoughtful. "If they're trying to disconnect me from your influence, I suppose they would have done."

"Reckon they knows 'ow 'elpful you are," Kez said. "'F I was them, I'd try to get rid av you, too."

"That's very comforting," muttered Tuan. "However, even if they've done something to the one that's connected to me, you're certain it's the death of your—your other friend that caused this one? Tuesday, Fifth World Orbiting Fuel Station?"

"Reckon," she said.

Tuan frowned down at the console. "Very well; I can do something about that."

"Wot you gunna do?" asked Kez, wandering back to hang over the console as well. "Gunna blow summink up?"

"Why on *earth* would I blow something up!"

"Blowin' stuff up is *fun*," Kez told him, disapprovingly. "You ain't no fun, TuanTuan."

"It might be fun, but there's no need for it in this case," Tuan said, keeping a wary eye on her. "We want to join things, not break them apart."

"Wot you lookin' at, anyway?" demanded Kez, craning to try and see the screen. Perhaps instinctively, Tuan had been shielding much of the screen from her.

"I'm looking for ways in," said Tuan. He moved slightly to one side—reluctantly, it seemed to Kez. "People we can use as a proxy; someone we can give a few extra memories to."

"'Ang on!" said Kez, chuckling deep in the back of her throat as she caught sight of a name on the screen. "'Ang on, TuanTuan! Go back! Wot's that one say, eh?"

"Sergeant Gormley, Evidence Collection. He signed in to the fuel station on that day and—"

"Ha!" Kez crowed. "Still around, is 'e?"

Tuan's eyes fastened on her sharply. "You know him? Perfect! That gives us a proxy! You can approach him and ask for his help —just don't go into specifics, or you'll risk breaking the Fixed Point all over again."

"'Ang on," interrupted Kez. "'E won't know me though. Not if Marx ain't 'ere."

"That's where I come in," said Tuan. "I've got an idea of what your Tuan did to bring the realities close enough to cross over. Enough so that we should be able to layer the two realities right next to each other. It won't quite do what your Tuan did—I suspect he's got a head-start on me in terms of software—but if I can pull them together for long enough, I can give this Sergeant Gormley your Sergeant's memories and get them to act in concert: the original and this one. If you've imprinted strongly enough on this Sergeant Gormley's memories, it shouldn't be a problem to give this reality's sergeant those memories."

"Yeah," said Kez, grinning. "Reckon that ain't a problem."

He looked at her suspiciously. "I'm not even slightly surprised. Well, it's all for the good, at least."

"'Ow do I get back, then? To me own reality?"

"You don't—not exactly. If everything goes right, and if my suspicions are correct, your own reality should come back to you: correcting the Fixed Point will zip up both sides of the fractured reality and make it one again with everything where it was to start with and a few extra bits. A few extra memories, too, maybe; I'm not quite sure about that bit."

Kez frowned. She often understood very little of what Tuan-Tuan said when he was talking about things he was enthusiastic about. "So wot, we're tryin' to kinda sew up the Fixed Point?"

"That is a *very rough* description of what we're doing," Tuan said severely. "It's barely accurate and highly unhelpful."

"Yeah, but I can understand it," Kez argued. "Told ya: I ain't got the brains. That's TuanTuan."

"So I see," Tuan said, sliding a look sideways at her. Kez rather thought he was smiling, and that was nice to see again.

"An' if we can get this bit all sewed back up again right and tight—"

"If we recalibrate the Fixed Point, it won't do any good for someone to try and unmake it a second time. By remaking it, we're making a Fixed Point of a Fixed Point, and anyone trying to unmake that would have to be mad or attempting to bring about the end of the Universe in one fell swoop. I don't know that it's even possible, because everything would be trying so hard to get back into the right place."

"Orright. So wot do we do? 'Ow do we get this version of the sergeant to remember me?"

"It should happen quite naturally if I get the calculation correct," he said. "I can't layer everything exactly, but I can do it for the span of today. Just one Tuesday. I'll be able to make a sort of corridor for you to walk between the two of them; you should be able to interact with both worlds, and hopefully influence your proxy to do what needs to be done."

"Right, corridor," said Kez, all at sea.

"I can only make a door into that corridor for a brief moment of time," he said; a warning. "I'll do it in the training module; it has some nice, strong locks on it."

Kez looked at him suspiciously. "You ain't gunna try to lock me in, are ya?"

"Good heavens, no! Would it do any good?"

"Nah."

"Why in heaven's name would I go to the effort for no result?"

"Fair enuff," said Kez, grinning. "Orright. I just go in 'ere, yeah?"

"That's right," he said, still typing away madly, a frown between his brows.

Kez stepped into the training module and the door sealed itself behind her. She was rather sure it locked itself after her, too. It was cold and hollow inside, and the room outside it looked slightly curved due to the maxiplex.

"Don't like it in 'ere," Kez said, and her voice echoed in a way that was somehow curved, too. "'Urry up, TuanTuan."

"I can't hurry," he murmured. "If I hurry, things will go wrong. You need to learn to be patient."

"Don't even," muttered Kez, but Tuan must have heard her, because she saw his lips curve as he stood over the console with his head ducked to read the screen.

And despite his warning, it seemed to Kez that his fingers began to type more and more quickly, flying over the keyboard while he seemed to hold his breath. It was just like TuanTuan to get so enthused in what he was doing that he did everything at super-speed, but she felt as though there was a new urgency to his work, and that made her worried—and thus, annoyed.

When a cold stillness sprang up around her, limning the inside of the training module, that crabbed annoyance made her grumble, "It's *cold*, TuanTuan."

He gave a breathy sort of laugh and turned from the console

to look at her properly through the maxiplex, one hand resting against it.

"Make sure you go when the light stops flashing," he said, tilting his chin up toward the light that was now flashing above her. "Just shift into the Other Zone and come back at exactly the same time, but somewhere close to your sergeant. When the light is solid, it's time to go. If you don't go then, and the connection is lost, I won't be able to do this again."

"'Ow come?"

"Whatever happens, go as soon as the connection occurs," Tuan said again, his eyes steadily on her. "Don't stop; don't look back."

"Wot you talkin' about?"

Why hadn't she seen it before: his hand up behind his ear, tugging on the hair there?

"TuanTuan!" Kez said, more sharply. "Wot you talkin' 'bout?"

"They've found me," he said. "I needed the power, so I was a bit too free with the mains system and they've picked up on the double versions of me."

"You'd better come wiv me, then," Kez told him. She hadn't meant to say that: he couldn't take over her TuanTuan's life. But something had to be done—some way could be found. And when everything zipped up again, or was sewn up again, he would disappear anyway, leaving only her TuanTuan in his place.

Kez's eyes grew dark and pebbly: whether or not he was her TuanTuan, that thought made her sad and *angry*.

"I'll come back out," she said. "Move us to a diff'rent place, yeah?"

"I think not," Tuan said. "Once you shift through that lot, it's all up; you'll be pulling the realities together. I'd rather you did it at the right time and made use of it. At the moment, it's only security coming. Besides, if I'm manning the mains out here, it'll take them longer to get into the room."

"You gunna be all right out there?"

"I should think so," he said. "They're not bringing along the beastie, at any rate: and they'll be more careful with me once they see I haven't got on the collar. You might think you can kick me with impunity, but I doubt they'll think so."

"Yeah, but I reckon they might shoot you," Kez said.

"I've sealed the door," he said. "By the time they manage to get it open, you should be gone. Make the most of it, Kez."

"*'Course*," she said. The tube of maxiplex around her went suddenly black, obscuring her view of the room, and Kez yelped. "Oi! Wot's goin' on? TuanTuan, wot you doin'?"

"It'll be better if they can't see you," said Tuan's voice, reasonable and even.

He didn't sound worried, but Kez's last vision of him, one hand pinching at the hair behind his ear, was burned brightly into the blackness of the maxiplex.

She waited, shivering, and thought she could hear the sound of Tuan's breath, soft and too quick, but perhaps it was just her own heartbeat. Then the sound of the outer door swishing open sounded in the module, surprisingly loud to be coming through only via Tuan's comm to the pod's speaker. Things were starting.

Kez bounced on her feet a little, her eyes flicking up to the light: it was still flashing.

"Here you are," said a voice through the comms, as if from a distance.

"Here I am," Tuan said, his voice echoing through the module with great clarity. "What do you want? I'm busy."

"That's interesting," the first voice said. "Because we just had confirmation that you're busy upstairs, as well. And that version of you has a collar on. What are we supposed to do with that?"

Tuan laughed. "That version of me, as well as you, and you, and *you*, and Auntie Li, can get—"

The sound of light discharge weaponry singed the air and crackled around the module. Kez heard a gasp, then a groan, and the sound of Tuan falling, perhaps to his knees.

"TuanTuan," she said, in a hushed voice. "Oi. TuanTuan. Get up."

"See to the console," said the same faint, unfamiliar voice. "Get it open. I don't know what he's got in there, but it's pulling time and reality out of place. If we don't stop this, Auntie Li will have our heads."

"She'll have our heads if you've killed him," said another voice.

"Not this time," said the first voice, and Kez heard Tuan give a small, snuffly laugh. "Uncle Cheng offered a good deal: she said he's collateral, this time. If he moves, kill him."

"Kez," said Tuan's voice in her ear, breathless and laboured. "There's another Fixed Point you're going to have to worry about now if you want to put everything back together. They'll go for that one for sure, after this."

"Tell me 'bout it when I get back from zippin' stuff up," Kez said mulishly. "Don't wanna know right now."

He laughed, thready and wet at the same time. "I'm not going to be here when you get back, Kez. That Fixed Point you said is attached to me—there are some memories coming back from the institute. Some things in my head that shouldn't be there. If your Tuan didn't have a collar, that's where it started."

"Stoppit, TuanTuan," Kez said uncertainly. "You're gunna help me wiv that one, too. I'll get back real quick, promise. It'll take a bit av *time* for the universe to zip back together, see? I'll come back and get ya: make sure I come back before they shoot ya, like."

"The Institute," he said again, his voice weaker than before, "where we should have met and didn't. That's where—that's where—"

Kez screamed in rage and kicked the maxiplex, but it barely made a sound on her side. On the other, it must have been altogether soundless, because she didn't hear the security men react. She could hear them through Tuan's comms, some of them still trying to find a way into the training module; some of them complaining about having shot Tuan too quickly.

"Save me, Kez," said Tuan breathlessly. "Save the other one of me that's worth saving."

She heard someone in the background say, "He's communicating with someone, sir!" then Tuan gasped once more and was silent.

Above, the light stopped flashing and glowed, continuous and strong.

Kez shifted in space, wrapped in a sticky, extra *something* that followed her and trailed its edges through the Other Zone; and with rage in her heart, she brought herself back into reality in the quarters of one Sergeant Gormley.

One Sergeant Gormley who, now that Kez had arrived, bringing with her another, sticky reality, would have to pass through a state of being *two* Sergeant Gormleys before he could hope to return to unification.

It was time to zip up an unzipped Fixed Point.

FALLOUT

It was early morning, and Lieutenant Tuan Li had just sat up in bed, yawning. There was nothing very much to be done today, so Tuan allowed himself to stretch and sit where he was for a few sleepy moments longer, wondering when the lingering sense of melancholy that clung to him would dissipate.

He yawned and pushed back the slightly-too long hair from his eyes, then stretched once more. As he did so, a pair of small, wiry arms wrapped themselves around his neck, nearly strangling him in their enthusiasm, and across the room, something small and piercing said *ting!* as it registered a presence for which it continuously searched.

A broad, glad, utterly joyful smile spread across Tuan's face, banishing the melancholy in a moment.

"Kez!" he said. "Why are you strangling me? You can't keep going back to times before I know you and then coming to strangle me for things I did when I didn't know you."

"Ain't stranglin' you," said the sharp, snubby voice he knew so well. "I'm *huggin'* you."

"Oh?" he said invitingly. This was a younger version of Kez, perhaps only a year after she'd met him for the first time, and if he was not mistaken, a more-than-usually traumatised version of her. "What happened? You can sit next to me, you know; tell me what happened."

"No," she said, clinging tighter. "Ain't lettin' you go."

"You might as well get used to it," said a male voice, from across the room. "She's probably going to perch there for the rest of the day."

There was Marx, short and nuggety, with his usual grease-stained coveralls and tough, stubbly face. Tuan very nearly asked him what he'd done to Kez, but since that would probably have called down punitive measures from Kez as well as her protector, and Kez was still very close to all of his main arteries, he refrained.

"What happened?" he asked, instead. He would have patted Kez on the head, but she avoided his hand and tucked her head in to bite his shoulder instead. Tuan said a mild "Ouch," more from habit than conviction, and heard a small snuffle from the general vicinity of his left ear.

Since it didn't seem likely that she was about to let go any time soon, Tuan gave up on his original plans for the morning—plans such as having a shower and getting dressed—and got up to wander across the room toward his small kitchen. He'd bought a package of red gummy frogs for just such an occasion: Kez loved soft textures to touch, and gummy textures to chew on. If given both, she was inclined to linger and even chat in her scattershot way, perfectly content to pull on his hair and natter in his ear, whether or not he was listening.

It wasn't a surprise to find that Marx had disappeared when Tuan turned around with Kez still clinging to his back.

Of Kez, he asked again, "What happened?"

"TuanTuan," she said in his ear, her voice scratchy, "reckon you could stop dyin' an' stuff?"

Tuan might have been chilled if it wasn't for the warmth clinging around his neck.

"I'm alive," he said to her. Kez at this age was far too fragile for anything but gummies and soft fabrics, and the few, soothing words that a person might say to a skittish Fifth World fleece-bird perched on one's shoulder and far too easily spooked into pooping.

"Yeah," she said in his ear. "Saved ya."

"Oh," he said, wriggling the bag of red gummy frogs in the general direction of his left shoulder. "Are you sure I didn't help you with that? Ow!"

This time, she bit him harder. A moment later, a skinny arm snaked out and grabbed a fist-full of red frogs, and Tuan couldn't help smiling. He wasn't bleeding, and Kez was eating; a fairly good sign that she was beginning to calm down.

"All right," he said. "You did it by yourself. You can tell me about it while I clean."

There was the sound of gummy chewing near Tuan's right ear, and one arm gripped more tightly as the other hand was fully engaged with a handful of gummy frogs, the elbow of that arm digging into his shoulder.

He tried to think of it as a rather more rabid form of massage, and began his day-off cleaning to the accompaniment of a series of raspberry-scented questions.

"Wot's that?"

"It's a duster."

"Hungry beggar, ain't it?"

...

"Wot's that?"

"A handheld dry-cleaner."

"It's makin' weird noises."

"It's just talking to me."

"'F someone dropped a gummy in there—"

"Don't drop a gummy in my dry-cleaner."

"Orright. But next time I'm gunna. Wanna see if it burps."

And finally, after Tuan had gone through his tiny living room, kitchen, and bathroom one by one, there was another huff of raspberry gummy air over his shoulder.

"Glad you ain't dead, TuanTuan."

THE MARRIAGE OF MIKKEL

MIKKEL HADN'T EXPECTED TO GET MARRIED. HE HAD expected, like many other Time Corp officers, that he would remain wedded to the job until retirement age; by which time he would be too old and set in his ways to settle down with anything other than a dog or a particularly patient robot.

It was somewhat stunning, therefore, at the relatively early age of thirty-eight, to find himself waiting in the special transport carrier that was to carry himself and his newly married wife back to his ship.

Traditionally, this would be the time when he would introduce her to his quarters, his men, and his ship. That made Mikkel snort just a bit. He doubted there was an area of his ship his bride didn't know better than he did—up to and including his quarters—and he was quite sure she had either bribed or threatened most of his men at some point.

Still, one had to observe the formalities.

"What's wrong?" asked a voice that still made Mikkel's heart jump.

Arabella, tidy but for the curls that never quite seemed to stay in place in her bun, slipped out of the bathroom and manoeuvred around him with the same deceptive ease that she always did, despite a form that was both plump and petite.

Mikkel very greatly appreciated that plump and petite figure; he also had a rueful appreciation for how quickly Arabella could best him in any kind of physical confrontation.

"Nothing at all," he said, turning to slip his arms around her. "Life is as close to perfect as I could hope for, as a matter of fact."

Arabella allowed the embrace and returned it with heart-warming strength, but when he tried to kiss her she turned her head and let his lips graze her cheek instead. She gently freed herself as well, and his heart dropped.

"You're going to ruin my hair, I think," she said. "And I really need it to be tidy for just a little while longer. I'm afraid I have to leave you alone now, Mikkel."

She turned to go while he was still frozen with the suddenness of it all, and Mikkel caught her wrist, surprised by a wild panic that sprang up, swift and overwhelming. He had expected so much more time before she had to be off again on errands for her shadowy employers.

Carefully light, he asked, "Regretting it already?"

"No," she said. "An er, important appointment is upcoming. I'll be back."

"An appointment?" Mikkel knew how that went: Arabella was with him until she wasn't. That was the way it had been since he'd met her. She could stay by his side for months, assisting him here and there with his own work and using him to assist, he was quite sure, with hers. Then she would be off again; off for a day, or a week, or a few months. It was always somehow approved in the system and the logs, but Mikkel didn't know how: he wasn't the one approving her secondments to other ships or organisations.

"A necessary one," she said, freeing her wrist from Mikkel's grasp to ineffectually smooth back the errant hairs that curled around her ears. "You know how sensitive these things are."

"I thought you'd at least stay for the wedding night," he said quietly as she turned once more to leave.

Arabella stopped and stared at him. "I think you may have gotten the wrong idea," she said. "I'll be back very shortly. This appointment is necessary but not lengthy: I'll be back before the transport starts moving."

"We haven't even picked out pet names," protested Mikkel. He knew it was no good, but he felt as though he had to do everything possible to stretch out the time with her. Perhaps part of him didn't really expect her to come back. "Don't you think we should settle on that before you go trotting off to appointments?"

"If I can't have my wedding night before the appointment, what on earth makes you think we've time to decide on pet names?" Arabella said, laughing. "Tell me what you've decided when I get back."

"I haven't even told you my Core password," he said, aware that he was very nearly pleading. "Is it such an important meeting? Can't your employers wait another day or two?"

Arabella hesitated—hesitated, and, he thought, smiled slightly. "Tell me that when I get back, too," she said, as if she had struggled with herself for a moment before coming to that answer.

She exited then, just as he'd known she eventually would, and Mikkel was left to loose his sighs upon the room.

"Reckon we should say congrats or summink," opined Kez.

There was a gleam to her eyes, so Marx said with finality, "Absolutely not. Tuan already said that we have to be careful how we approach them, and if you think I want to clean wedding cake off the ceiling, you've got another think coming."

"E only said we gotta be careful 'bout bein' friendly wiv 'em," objected Kez. "Ain't ever been exactly friendly, 'ave we?"

"I'm not the one who stabbed him," Marx pointed out. "And besides that, there isn't a man alive who wants to be bothered on his wedding day. We've managed pretty well with Mikkel so far, but if we disturb him today, he's likely to turn nasty later."

Kez mumbled, "Maybe we can just set off a cracker or summink. So they know we're thinkin' of 'em."

"Listen, kid: if I knew you were thinking about me, I wouldn't be able to sit down without twitching. Leave them alone."

There was a rather sulky silence, then Kez brightened. "Oi," she said. "Forgot! We already said hi."

There was only so long that he could sit sighing at the ceiling, so Mikkel eventually rose to make himself a cup of coffee and pinch some of the icing off the wedding cake. Everything they needed had been loaded into the transporter—it would also, if tradition were to be followed, take the long way around on the way back to the ship.

He would have taken a bite of that cake, but he was fairly sure Arabella would have something to say about it if he tasted it without her. It was safer to refrain. Arabella was very fond of chocolate: particularly chocolate and orange together, and this cake had both.

Still, he couldn't be expected to wait for mere *icing*, and as the coffee maker did its little burbling thing, Mikkel swiped a decent amount of it from the edge of the plate. Since it paired well with the sip of coffee he had afterward, he repeated the happy accident after filling his cup.

Engaged in so doing, Mikkel didn't hear the hatch open, but when he turned at a whisper of sound, cup of coffee in one hand and licking the icing from his forefinger, Arabella was back again. She looked as though she had come back in a hurry, too: her cheeks were slightly flushed, and there were a few more curls floating free than there had been several minutes earlier.

"Forget something, did you?" he asked. "Or is your appointment later than you expected?"

"The appointment?" asked Arabella, twisting her marriage ring on her finger. "Oh yes; didn't I tell you it was a short one?"

"I didn't start the cake without you," he said guiltily.

A smile sprang to her lips, and as soon as he saw that smile, Mikkel knew it wasn't just her hair that seemed so different. That smile was the first real, spontaneous emotion he had seen from her since she came back into the room. Arabella had always been straightforward and reasonably comfortable with him, so he hadn't realised how much more comfortable and straightforward she had become with him over the two years he'd known her, until he saw her again now as she had been when he first met her.

This Arabella, just slightly off balance—and wearing, he now noticed, a *very* slightly older version of the Time Corp hat she had been wearing just a few minutes earlier—was not the Arabella who had just married him. This Arabella was a younger Arabella; two years younger, if he was correct.

"We can save it for later," she said. "But if you happen to have another cup of coffee at hand—"

"Always, for you," said Mikkel, and filled a second mug. From the corner of his eye, he saw her sit down on the couch, and said affably, "Why don't we use the love-seat? It's a bit more cosy, don't you think? And they put it in here just for us—it isn't requisition for transporters."

He could have imagined the very faint sigh that huffed out in the cool air, but Mikkel didn't think so. Nevertheless, Arabella changed seats, the blue of her dress uniform dusky against the white faux fur, and settled herself as far back as possible in it. Not to take advantage of what seemed, frankly, a very uncomfortable curved chair arm, thought Mikkel, but to remain as far away from him as possible.

Mikkel watched that in the reflection of the tiny galley's faux-tiles, then banished his grin and turned with both mugs.

As he did, she said, "I just remembered that you haven't given me your code yet."

"Ah, the code," said Mikkel; startled, disbelieving, and fascinated.

For the first time since he had met Kez and Marx, he felt that he finally understood what was happening. More: he understood his own part in it. The exhilaration of that understanding brightened the smile that had sprung to his lips, and the deepening flush of red across the younger Arabella's cheeks at that smile set his heart thundering in his ears.

Not just today, but when they first met, she had loved him.

For Mikkel, who had never been sure where her job for her mysterious employers left off and where her (hopefully) real regard began, it was a balm to the soul.

And today, he was quite certain, *today*, she had come for the single purpose of finding out his Core password: that code that was particular to him and to be shared with no-one but a legally bound partner who would be considered by the Time Corp as one and the same as himself.

Right now, this Arabella, under compulsion from two rogue time travellers, was here to pilfer from him his Core password—and how she would go about doing that was something he was very curious about.

"You're always so business-minded," he said as he sat down, playfully reproachful. He made sure to sit closer to her than to his own armrest; close enough to feel the warmth of his arm against hers. Close enough so that when he leaned forward to put her cup of coffee on her side of the coffee table, he briefly felt her breath tickle the hair at his temples.

There was no reason for him not to have a bit of fun with the interview: both of them knew what she was here for, but for what felt like the first time since he'd known her, Mikkel felt that he had the advantage—two, in fact. Firstly, he knew the outcome of this particular situation. Secondly, although Mikkel knew what Arabella had come for, she didn't know that he knew.

Testingly, he added, "You haven't even given me a kiss since the ceremony. A husband might take that in a bad sort of way."

Arabella chuckled suddenly, a small, warm thing in the back of her throat. "Are you telling me that your Core password can be purchased for a kiss? How would your superiors feel about that?"

"They don't try to kiss me," Mikkel said, grinning. He edged forward again, the coffee cups comfortably out of the way, and nudged a small kiss just below her ear. "So they're not likely to find out."

She cleared her throat very slightly. "I suppose that's something, then," she said. To his delight, her breathing had quickened just slightly; nor, he saw, had she tried to back further away from him. Instead, she leaned forward and planted a small, hesitant sort of kiss on his cheek.

Mikkel didn't give her a chance to pull back: he ducked his

head and kissed the lips that were so close, aware of the two hands that presently grasped his shirt-collars.

If he had entertained any doubts at all about which Arabella it was he was kissing, that kiss would have allayed them thoroughly. Arabella, Mikkel had learned very quickly, was alert under any circumstance whatsoever. This included those circumstances in which she might be forgiven for having her thoughts focused otherwhere: up to and including a certain stiffness while occupied in kissing, due to an apparently innate need to keep an eye on her surroundings.

The Arabella he had married that morning no longer had any stiffness whatsoever. For all Mikkel knew, she maintained that alertness in a less noticeable way; however, these days, she seemed to trust Mikkel enough to at least allow him to take some share of the watch during an embrace of any sort, and it had consequently become easier to kiss her.

"No one is going to come through the hatch or the portholes," he said to her. "The hatch should be locked by now, and if the portholes are open, we'll have more issues than a couple of interlopers."

"I wasn't particularly worried about people coming through the hatch or portholes," said Arabella, her eyes flickering around the room.

Mikkel managed to suppress the grin that was trying to form, and leaned a little closer to the younger version of his wife. "I've got the feeling that no one will disturb us for a little while yet," he said. "Everyone knows there are ten digits to a Core password, and I'm sure they expect an exchange for every digit."

Arabella looked momentarily taken aback. "They?"

"My men don't expect us back on the *Slider* for at least another hour or so," explained Mikkel, enjoying himself very much. "In fact, I'll be very surprised if they expect us in less than three hours."

Arabella's eyes began to dance. "Oh, is that how it works? A kiss for every digit?"

"Yes," said Mikkel, very firmly. "And if it's not tradition, we'll make a new one."

"I'm shocked," Arabella said, somewhat piously, "that I've given the impression as a wife that I'll be less than forthcoming with kisses." She kissed him beside the mouth. "It's not—" a kiss on the other side, "—at all representative—" a third kiss by his ear "—of me."

His face cupped in two small, capable hands, Mikkel gazed down at Arabella and was surprised by a fourth kiss that fell squarely on his lips.

"That makes five," said Arabella, sitting back with a laugh in her eyes and a flush still over her cheeks. "Seven, if you count the one you stole first and the one after that."

"We're not counting those two," Mikkel told her.

"Very well," said Arabella, capturing one of his hands between hers. In quick succession, she kissed that hand four times, the last kiss landing on the inside of his wrist before he pulled himself away.

Reproachfully, Mikkel said, "That's *cheating*."

"Last one," said Arabella, eyes alight with laughter, but mouth rueful.

"Then this one is mine to take," he countered. If he was only going to get one last chance to kiss this adorable version of his wife—that Arabella he had so often wanted to kiss in the past—Mikkel was going to make sure he did the thing thoroughly.

"Flaming heck," said Marx, drawing in a breath through his teeth. "I nearly forgot about that."

That particular incident had been about a year ago, if you went by his and Kez's particularly fractured timeline: they had desperately needed a Core password to stay one step ahead of the Time Corp, and since their timeline interacted sporadically with Mikkel's—and in increasingly disparate parts of that timeline—they had been aware of the marriage for at least the last two years. It had made sense at the time to use

Arabella to winkle a Core password out of Mikkel without anyone being the worse for it, and without Mikkel feeling that he had to report the breach.

Marx had always wondered how much Mikkel understood of what happened that day. Their timelines had been reversed for the events that led up to the stealing of the password; what was and wasn't known, and by whom, had been a bit hard to gauge by the time everything was done. Only Kez seemed to be completely unfazed by it all, though Marx had never been sure that she would know how to deal with a strictly linear timeline anyway.

"That's today, is it?" he said. "That makes it a year and a half that we've been running around together, doesn't it?"

"Yeah," said Kez. She had a mouthful of something, and Marx had a momentary flash of the same instinct that would have prompted him to scruff a dog and force its mouth open to get rid of whatever disgusting object it had found beneath a bush somewhere.

Fortunately for the both of them, the scent of raspberry hit his nostrils a moment later.

He sent a hard look in her direction. "You've been visiting Tuan again, haven't you?"

Kez stopped chewing. "Ay?"

"I already saw you chewing. I told you not to go visiting the kid until later on: if we go to see him too often, they'll get the idea that he's a bit too close to us. We've apparently already had to repair a Fixed Point to make sure you meet up with him."

"Got these from 'im last time," she clarified, through a mouthful of gummy frog. "He gave me a whole packet."

"Wonderful," muttered Marx.

"Oi," said Kez. "You're pretty flamin' nice for a bloke who didn't remember to say summink when you'd had me for a year."

"You want me to celebrate the one year anniversary of picking up a feral little girl who keeps kicking me and steering my ship into goat houses?"

"It was only one goat house," mumbled Kez. "An' it looked nice sittin' up there on our nose."

"*You didn't remember, either,*" Marx pointed out.

"*Did so too! Gave you a present an' everyfink!*"

"*A prese—are you trying to tell me that letting a full-size twenty-first century anaconda into my bunk was an anniversary present?*"

"*It was just a baby,*" complained Kez. "*An' it just wanted to 'ave a bit av kip next to ya all warm like.*"

"*It was measuring itself up against me when I woke up,*" Marx said, without mincing matters. "*Straight as a ruler. And what's more, it was twice the length of me.*"

"*You didn't 'ave to go caperin' about the ship because o'that!*"

"*Listen, kid; when a snake measures itself up against a person, it's because it's trying to see if it's big enough to swallow that person. Where did you get it?*"

"*Some bloke in an 'at.*"

"*Well, stop consorting with blokes in hats. And stop introducing creatures into—kid.*"

"*Yeah?*"

"*Did you send Mikkel and Bells a wedding present?*"

"*Wot you lookin' at me like that for?*"

Marx leaned forward and looked directly into those glittering black eyes. "*Kez.*"

"*Well,*" said Kez. "*Figgered I should get 'em somefink.*"

Mikkel had wondered, somewhere in the back of his mind that wasn't occupied with kissing, exactly what Arabella would use as an excuse to get away once he had told her his Core password. She couldn't very well make an exit straight away without looking as though she really had been there only for the password, but she couldn't very well stay much longer without going beyond the scope of what she had come to do. Mikkel was also very much aware that the longer Arabella stayed, the harder it was to stop at merely kissing her: it was one of the reasons he had told her his Core password before he kissed her for the last time.

It was much to his mixed regret and relief, therefore, that a ship-wide, all-comms call went out for Arabella to attend the engine room, somewhere between the time he began to kiss her for the last time and the point at which he would have thought it good to stop.

"What in the Twelve Known Worlds do this think they're playing at?" demanded Mikkel, sitting up again in wrathful surprise. They weren't even aboard their own ship: moreover, they were only waiting for clearance for their transporter. "Stay where you are; I'll ask them what they think they're doing."

"Never mind," Arabella said, scooting away from him and rising from the love-seat with some haste. "I think I'd better go see what they want. If I don't think they've a good enough reason to bother us, I'll give them a good talking to, you can be sure."

"I'll expect more kisses when you come back!" Mikkel called after her, regret and delight vying for prominence. Had she set it up previously, or could he thank Kez and Marx for that as well?

He sat back on the couch, laughter making a warm ball in his chest, and waited for the hatch to open once again. It opened less than ten seconds after it closed behind the younger Arabella, a pleasant surprise that also afforded him a great deal more amusement than it should have.

"You're back!" he said affably, as the hatch closed and emitted a short beep to indicate that the transporter had been cleared for departure. "To stay, this time, I should hope!"

Arabella crossed the room and hit his shoulder with a sharp, short blow that sounded much worse than it was, and Mikkel was surprised into laughter.

"Is that something you should be doing to your brand new husband?" he protested, in spite of that.

"My darling," said Arabella, making the breath catch in his throat, "might I remind you that I have all of the memories of what you've been doing while I've been gone?"

"I wondered," Mikkel began, bright and exhilarated, "I

always wondered who it was that had made you so flushed when you went off to get that code. And I was almost certain it was my code you went to get."

"Now you know," she said, divesting herself of her uniform jacket and settling herself on his lap.

"The cheek of it," he said virtuously, slipping his arms around her so that she couldn't go away again. "Seducing a married man on his wedding day!"

"I actually thought until today that you didn't know it was the younger me," Arabella said, grinning. The transporter began to move with a slight jar, and she steadied herself against his shoulders. "I thought I'd done so well to get your code in a way that couldn't come back to hurt you! Of course, as soon as I walked back in here and saw you looking so happy and pleased with yourself, I knew otherwise."

"You were so adorable," he said.

"I felt dreadful about it!" she protested. "It didn't occur to me that you would put it all together like that. If you knew *then*, why didn't you...?"

"I didn't know," he said. "Not certainly enough to make a report about it. And I didn't know for sure until you came in just before with the older soft hat instead of this year's."

Arabella laughed again. "That dreadful little child! No wonder she was so happy with herself! She knew about the hat, but she didn't tell me: all she would tell me was that I'd eventually marry you and that I needed to pretend to be your wife for long enough to get the code. Of course, I already knew that, but—"

"One moment," interrupted Mikkel, rising and drawing her toward the couch instead of the love-seat. There was more room on the couch, and he didn't think Arabella would be trying to edge away from him this time. "What do you mean, you already knew that?"

"My employers know a great deal about the future that even Kez and Marx don't know," she said, allowing herself to be drawn and sitting down within a pleasing proximity. "I've known since I came to work with you. I hadn't made up my mind, of course, but I was open to the possibility."

Mikkel put his arm around her and bent his head to trail a series of soft kisses from her collar-bone to her ear. "What made you open to the possibility?"

"Your delightfully broad chest, naturally," she said, turning a little in his arms to lay a warm hand on that chest. "And your golden curls, of course."

She touched one of those, too, but dropped the hand back to his chest where it created a swiftly growing patch of warmth.

"Didn't they give you a picture of me to win you over?" he asked her.

"Of course," she said. "But it's one thing to see it in a picture, and quite another to experience the grandeur of it in person for the first time. Distracting, one could say."

"I didn't notice that you were particularly distracted at the time," Mikkel said. "You sent me to the mat without a blink."

"Pure shyness, sir."

There was an awful pause before he said incredulously, "Did you just *sir* me again?"

"You were the one who told me to think of a pet name!" she protested, but Mikkel was quite sure her protests were spurious.

"I preferred it when you were calling me *my darling*," he said.

"Kez," said Marx, his mind rebelling from the immediate idea that had presented itself to him. "That bloke in a hat—he wasn't doing a two for one sale, was he?"

"Yeah," she said. "Got Bells an' Golden Boy a present at the same time."

"You put an anaconda on the wedding gift table?"

"Nah," said Kez, at first relieving his mind considerably. Then she added, "Put the present straight in their room. Didn't want anyone else to pinch it."

Marx closed his eyes. "You put an anaconda in their quarters?"

"Nah," she said again.

"You're a rollercoaster ride, kid," said Marx, opening his eyes. He didn't dare to hope.

"Said 'e didn't 'ave two snakes, but he gave me summink else instead. Summink just as good."

"At this rate, one of us has to be put out of our misery," Marx said, at the ceiling. "Kid. What did you put in Golden Boy's room?"

"Dunno," said Kez. "But it 'ad a lotta tentacles an' a nice smile. And it don't need water so they can keep their bath. Marx! Where you goin', Marx?"

OTHER ZONE ANIMAL INCURSION, LEVEL FOUR.

The incursion occurred Onboard Relative Time <redacted> aboard the *TCS Slider*. Alarms were raised when Captain Mikkel of the *TCS Slider* was awakened by swiftly tightening tentacles from a Deep Other Zone animal that had made its way into the timestream by means unknown and was attempting to return and take with it a convenient meal.

Fortunately for Captain Mikkel and his new wife, who removed the animal from his vicinity by use of a sedative and a pair of tongs, the beast was too small to have drawn anyone other than a small child back into the Other Zone. The animal was ejected from the ship via the nearest safe porthole, where it was picked up by Incursion Specialist Team #3, who expedited its return to the Other Zone.

Witnesses to Incursion: *None*
Witnesses to Source of Incursion: *Two; both human*
Witnesses to Retrieval: *None*
Risk Assessment: *Negligible; animal was never identified*
Recommended Action: *Check all marketplaces twice a month to prevent the sale of such Other Zone Animals to unsuspecting customers; ensure that all such animals are returned as promptly as possible to give no chance for said animals to infiltrate Time Corp Vessels*

SPORK INCLUDED

"It sez," said Kez, "spork included. Lookit. Right there. An' if it sez that, it should be in there."

"Don't know what to tell you, kid," Marx said, without turning away from the console. "It's not there. What are you going to do about it?"

"Well, I fort we might go and visit 'em at the factory. Got a bit av that plastic explosive left, an'—"

"We're not blowing up a tuckbox factory because they didn't give you a spork in your tuckbox."

"Not all of it," protested Kez. "Just the bit wot does the recon-reconstitutated plastics. They gotta learn that they can't go pinchin' someone else's spork."

"If somebody pinched your spork, I doubt it was some poor sap in the factory," Marx told her. "Kid, if you kick my chair once more—!"

Kez glared at him, and as if he felt the molten influence of that stare, Marx finally looked across at her.

"I'm concerned," Kez told him. "If they ain't doin' a proper job includin' the sporks, wot else are they gunna do?"

"At the very least, I doubt they're likely to blow anyone up," Marx said. "Listen, kid; we're neck deep in trying to avoid Time Corp and the Core's gone mucky enough to make me think that someone's messing with us—"

"Make a nice 'oliday, eh?" Kez said persuasively. "Summink fun to do to clear the cobwebs out, right?"

"I don't think finding you a spork counts as necessary work," said Marx. "Some people would even say it's a mercy not to have to use one."

"Them people prob'ly ain't tried to eat a tuckbox," opined Kez. "They're prob'ly rich an' stuff. I want me spork! I'm flamin' hungry!"

"Fine," said Marx. "We'll find you a spork. But we're not blowing anything up."

"Not a spork," said Kez stubbornly. "My spork. The one wot they said was included."

Marx stared at her for a thoughtful few seconds. At last he said, "I don't know why I'm always dragging terriers around with me."

"'Zat mean we're gunna get my spork?"

"All right, all right, just don't bite anyone."

There was a red dot blinking on a small screen at Mikkel's console when he woke up. He didn't like red dots on his console in general, but he liked red dots even less when they were on this screen in particular.

Groaning, he rolled out of bed, and slapped a hand onto the communicator that was waiting within arm's reach.

"We're on alert," he said, his voice still rough with sleep. "Kez and Marx just popped up again."

When he strode out into the passageway, still pulling on his uniform jacket, Arabella was already waiting for him; probably had been for some time already.

Mikkel sent a somewhat sour look in her direction. "If you're planning on shutting me in my room or hitting me on the head or—"

"Just here to help, sir," she said soothingly.

"To help *whom* exactly? Those employers of yours? Yourself?"

"Don't be like that, sir. Ostensibly, my employers are Time Corp."

"Yes," said Mikkel, trying vainly to straighten his collar at the back. "That's exactly what I'm complaining about. *Ostensibly.* Ostensibly, I'm a high-functioning and well-decorated officer— no one knows that I'm actually a complete wreck just waiting for the day when those two finally derail my career beyond repair."

"You're not a wreck, sir," Arabella said comfortingly, rising on tiptoes to fix the collar for him.

Her hands were warm and firm, and Mikkel, distracted from the urgency of his mission by the fact that Arabella was equally warm and very much within arm's reach, had to remind himself not to put his arms around her.

"And why do you always arrive so early?" he complained. It was unfair of her to be so firm and business-like about his collar when he found it so appallingly difficult to resist slipping his arms around her. "The first time I met you, I was just getting out of the shower; now that you're *ostensibly* working for me, there's never an incident with those two where you don't turn up while I'm still getting dressed or just getting out of bed."

Arabella smoothed his collar from the back to the front in one, swift, precise movement, and for the briefest moment, Mikkel was aware of the tug of her hands as she gripped his collar.

"That would be because you're so adorable when you're half-dressed and frowsy, sir," said Arabella, with stunning forthrightness. She patted his chest once, then released him and started down the passageway toward the bridge.

"Wait!" Mikkel said, belatedly breaking free from his stupor. He strode down the passageway after her, calling, "Come back here!"

"Absolutely not, sir," said Arabella, walking just a little bit faster. "I have a feeling that might be more dangerous than an encounter with Kez and Marx. They're waiting for us on the bridge."

Kez had made no promises not to bite someone. She hadn't decided she *would* bite someone, but she liked to leave her options open. Sometimes biting happened on the spur of the moment: a necessary adjunct to a current situation.

Marx knew that, and in Kez's opinion his not reminding her again was tacit agreement that if the situation called for biting, biting was allowed. Kez herself would, of course, be the best judge of whether or not the situation called for biting.

Still, when they arrived at the production plant by the simple expedient of a quick Core search and an unused loading bay that was just big enough to house the *Upsydaisy*, it seemed that the point was moot. Marx had doctored his usual workman's identification to give them easier access, but there was no need to use it: not only was the loading bay completely unpeopled, the production floor stretched as long and empty as a desert ahead of them when they entered the double-doors at one end. A few drink-bottles stood beside some swivel seats along the conveyer belts as if the owners had merely gone to lunch, but the production floor itself was messy and cluttered. Kez had worked a few production lines in her short life, and she was aware that employees didn't leave for any kind of break without tidying the floor first.

It was needless to remark that the place was empty: Kez, however, in her annoyance, felt the need to draw attention to the fact.

"Ain't no one 'ere," she said disapprovingly. "No wonder there's problems in pro—in *pro*duction."

"Maybe they've gone to lunch," said Marx. "Listen, kid, empty is good."

He said that, but Kez was fairly certain he didn't mean it: he had that look to him, all sharp glances with just his eyes moving, and he had already positioned himself where he could see in all directions.

"Ain't," she said, shooting him a look of her own as she started up the room.

"Look," said Marx, grabbing a spork off the production line closest. "Here's a tuckbox spork. Time to take off."

"Ain't mine," said Kez, without stopping.

Marx's voice came from behind her, grey and hard. "What do you mean, *not mine?*"

"Ain't mine," Kez called, and broke into a trot. If Marx was too close, he would grab her and drag her back toward the *Upsy-daisy*, and even though she could slip out of his grasp by dodging through either time or space temporarily, that was *cheating* and not allowed unless necessary.

She heard him start to jog behind her—heard the muttered, Third World words he was using to swear—and hustled a bit faster, grinning. Kez could fairly smell mischief, and she wanted to know why that Mischief had deprived her of her spork when it was most needed. She kept up a good speed and used her smaller size to nip under things Marx had to go around, always just in the lead. She had only a vague conception of why he was so desperate to stop her from running wild in this particular facility—even Kez was aware that an empty facility was not a good sign—but even if he didn't want to investigate further, she *did*.

There was a snarl from behind her, and a threateningly low voice said, "Kid! Get back here! If I slip in *one* more puddle of tuckbox slop, I'm going to pack you off in your own tuckbox complete with a spork!"

"Can't," Kez said back, though he wouldn't be able to hear her from behind the gurgling tank she'd skirted. Her assertion was untrue, if one looked at it from a purely physical perspective. When one looked at it as a matter of principle, however, it was obvious that Kez couldn't do as she was told. "Gotta get me *spork*! Heck!"

This last exclamation was forced from her rather than said by her: Kez collided with a wall of sheer muscle that was as unperturbed by the collision as a real wall might have been, and bounced backward with some force.

She said "Heck!" again when she was able to draw breath, staring at the sheer height of the giant she had bounced off. Fascinated, she demanded, "Wot'd *you* stand in growin' up? I fort only weeds grew like that!"

The giant tilted his head at her without understanding—Seventh Worlder, Kez realised, belatedly, and possibly didn't understand Universal—then swooped and seized her by the collar.

Curious and not yet frightened—she had her ability to shift, and, more importantly, she had *Marx*—Kez allowed him to scruff her without doing more than grin offensively at him as she dangled from his huge hand.

The giant lifted her until he could take in the full effect of that offensive grin, and said in Seventh World dialect, "What is this little thing?"

"Bad luck," she told him, switching to dialect; and since the offensive grin wasn't having as much effect as she would have liked, she scowled at him. "Why didden you give me a spork, eh?"

"What?" he said, the word nasal and drawn out in dialect.

"Shoulda given me a *spork*," she said, more clearly. She could see Marx over the muscly shoulder: he tapped a finger to his lips and melted back into the conveyer belts and swivel seats of the production line. Again in dialect, she said, "Because then I wouldn't have *come*, and then you would've gotten away with all of this."

The giant froze, then shook her once more, this time until her teeth rattled. Through the fuzziness of the assault, Kez heard him growl, "What do you know about this, you little rat?"

Kez flung this way and that, instinctively curled into herself and wrapped her legs around that beam of an arm, snaking her arms around it as well, and thus twisted away from her collar, attached herself by the teeth for good measure.

He screamed, and would have shaken her off if he could, but Kez was firmly attached; legs, arms, and teeth. The giant spun in a circle, still viciously shaking his arm to fling her away from himself, and Kez saw a second man flash in and out of sight; heard the babble of his voice testily advising the giant to stop and *listen*. The giant did neither, and Kez, feeling her grip waver, did a small shift that let her pre-empt and soften the inevitable release, tumbling to a stop several feet from the giant.

He retreated a step, cradling the injured arm with his other arm, and the second man stepped forward. Like Marx, he seemed to be very well aware what Kez was capable of, because he seized her by the ear instead of the collar, his hand out of reach of her teeth.

Kez could have shifted once again, but now she was curious. There was something about being with Marx that gave her the space to be curious instead of biting, running, and hiding, and Kez liked having the space to be curious.

She was also still very much annoyed that her spork had been purloined.

The man who had a grip on her ear gave it a bit more of a pinch and said, "Listen, kid; where's the other one?"

"Summink wrong wiv yer eyes?" asked Kez solicitously.

"There is nothing wrong with my eyes. Where is the other one?"

"I look like two people to you, bucko?"

He twisted the ear, and Kez bared her teeth at him.

"Then who were you talking to before?

"Ain't a crime to talk to meself, is it?" she demanded, hunching her shoulders.

She heard the clicky pickup of a comm behind her, and the man with a grip on her ear said, "I hear you. Yeah, we've picked up a little rat out here. Want to see it, or should we throw it in the freezer with the others?"

The giant looked expectantly at the man behind her. "Well?"

"Freezer's full," he said. "Boss wants to see the kid: he says to bring it along."

Kez could have slipped away then and there, but Marx wasn't attacking anyone, which meant that things were safe enough for now. Besides, this factory had *promised* her a spork, she had *come* for her spork, and she was going to find out why she hadn't been *given* a spork. It was obvious that these Seventh Worlders knew something about the state of the production floor, and Kez was very much of the persuasion that punishing anyone but the perpetrators of wrong was a waste of energy.

"Come here, you," said the giant. Made cautious by past

experience, he grabbed her by the neck instead of the collar, where she couldn't bite him.

Kez only grinned at him, and that seemed to bother him, because he shuffled her until she was facing away from him. She grinned at the back of the second man instead.

First she would find out what they had done, and then she would know who to bite.

"Report!" barked Mikkel as he strode onto the bridge.

"We've got a code thirty-four that came in five RMUs ago," said the commander, pleasingly prompt.

Mikkel waited for him to continue, but the silence stretched out, thin and awkward. Eventually, he said impatiently, "Well? We've had six minutes notice now: where are we going?"

The commander and lieutenant exchanged glances before the lieutenant, always the more willing of the two to make a fool of himself, said, "We're not sure yet, sir. That is; we're pretty sure, but we're pretty sure about two different places, and *last* time something like this happened we went to the wrong one of the two places, so—"

Mikkel tried to hide the sigh that swelled his lungs, but wasn't quite successful in doing so. "Why do we have two locations again? I thought they found the glitch in the Core that made it look like those two were in two different places at once?"

"They did, sir," said Arabella, causing the commander and lieutenant to both shoot her an appreciative look. "I read the official memo: it's on your desk for today. The problem as far as I can tell is that the Core isn't quite sure yet exactly which version of events is going to happen."

"That's exactly it," said the commander, latching gratefully onto her explanation. "The Core is having trouble narrowing it down to one of two outcomes, and each outcome has a different place for the two of them to end up. It looks like one of them is still wavering back and forth about what decision they want to make."

"Or we've got another Core breach," Mikkel said, a little grimly.

"Well, yes sir."

"Either way, we have to wait and see."

"Yes sir."

"Make sure she's ready to go as soon as we know exactly where and when. And get a time lock ready to go: I don't want to hear that we've let them slip through our fingers because we couldn't get a time lock settled around the place as soon as possible."

From his side and slightly behind, Mikkel heard Arabella murmur, "And what will you do with them if you catch them, sir?"

He looked back at her, and was fairly certain that she was a hairsbreadth from laughter. Wanting to surprise it out of her, he said affably, "Oh, I don't suppose it'll go as far as that, do you?"

Arabella choked a little. "I thought you were quite determined this time, sir."

"I am," he said. "But I've yet to learn that my determination has any bearing on an outcome when it comes to those two. I just don't want to make stupid mistakes. If by some chance I *do* catch them one day, I fully expect it to be because they want to be caught, and I'll be living in constant fear until they're off my ship."

"I'm glad to see you so resigned, sir," she said. "If it helps, I'm rather sure that there will be a good outcome from this regardless of Kez and Marx."

"Are you?" he asked, highly suspicious. And then, as she went to assist the navigation officer to double up on co-ordinates, "A good outcome for who, that's what I'd like to know!"

. . .

Kez, dangling from one massive ham of a fist as her captor headed deeper into the building, amused herself by paddling with her feet and scanning the production floor to see if she could catch a glimpse of Marx. She didn't know what he was up to, but she was sure it was bound to be fun; more, she was certain he wouldn't leave her here alone.

Deeper into the factory was another set of double doors that were set up for decontamination. To Kez's indignation, the decontamination gear had been disassembled with some force: she didn't object to disassembling items with force, but she was very fond of the sudden, icy blast of decontamination spray and the following warm gush of clean air that dried and finished the process.

They passed through the doors without provoking more than a sulky hiss of escaping air from one of the decontamination units, and Kez heard the sound of conversation floating down the hall toward them. The cool wall of industrial fridges on one side, and the frosty edge of a walk-in freezer on the other side gave her the chill that she hadn't got from the decontamination unit, but when there was no following warmth of clean air, Kez became irritable.

"Don't go openin' the freezer!" she snapped at the man who had seized her by the ear. "It's flamin' cold!"

"Mind your manners, or you'll go in there yourself," he told her briefly, opening the door despite her snarl.

Over his shoulder, Kez caught a glimpse of people—no, she realised, looking into glassy eyes for a brief moment, *bodies*—and vigorously kicked the second man in the shoulder.

"Oi," she said. "Wot you lot fink you're doin'? You can't pack people into freezers. Even *I* knows that."

The giant shook her casually. "Shut up."

"We only put the dead ones in there," said another voice from down the hall. "If they behave, they stay in the fridge."

Kez turned her eyes away from the freezer and toward the fridge doors on the other side—which had, she now realised, locks on the outside of them. When she had looked at those, she turned an angry look on the man who had spoken. She had seen many pleasant-faced Seventh-Worlders: TuanTuan was one of them, with his curving, happy eyes and crooked smile. This Seventh-Worlder's eyes were as narrow as TuanTuan's were, but where TuanTuan's eyes were bright and sparkling, this man's were hard as black granite.

Almost, Kez thought, her own black eyes growing dark and pebbly, as dangerous as her own.

"'Oo are you, then?" she asked.

"Carrigan," he said, though he seemed surprised to find himself answering her.

Kez didn't think it was his real name—not unless he was third or fourth generation removed Seventh Worlder, changing his name to fit whatever world he'd settled in.

"'Oo'd you put in there?" she asked him, tilting her chin at the fridge door.

"The workers," he said. This time, Kez got the impression that he meant to answer her; that he meant to scare her. He said to the giant, "Bring her in. We're in the middle of a game and it's cold out here."

The giant followed him down the hallway and into the back room that seemed to be a staffroom, if the kitchen and chairs were anything to go by. Over his shoulder, Carrigan said to Kez, "They don't get to mischief if we keep them in the fridges, and by the time they get out, they're so grateful that they just work without giving us any problems."

He sat back down at a table with three others and picked up his cards, smiling pleasantly at her.

Kez said, conversationally, "Better get 'em outta there."

He huffed a very small laugh beneath his breath as he threw down a card. "Why?"

"'Cos they gives me sporks wiv me tuckbox, an' you lot don't."

"That sounds like a problem for you, but I don't see why it's my problem."

"That's why I said you better let 'em go," explained Kez. "'Cos right now it's my problem, but if you don't let 'em go, it's gunna be *yore* problem, gettit?"

This time Carrigan laughed aloud. "A very small problem. Throw her into the fridge with the others."

"It bit me," the giant pointed out.

"Then disinfect yourself. The freezer's nearly full, and we're still going to be here for a while. Put her in the fridge."

The giant scowled, but he seemed to be a well-trained giant; the worst he did was to toss Kez across the chilly floor of the fridge instead of allowing her to get there under her own impetus. She tumbled into the far wall, leaving a skid of boot-black and displaced ice, and someone detached from the huddled mass of people in the corner to help her up.

Kez scowled reflexively at the woman who helped her up before the rattling of the lock outside the fridge reminded her that the enemy was outside, not inside. She tried grinning instead, but that only made the woman say uncertainly, "It hurt, didn't it? It's just because it's so cold in here. Come over with the others and we'll get you warmed up."

"Ain't cold," said Kez. "Ain't hurt, either."

The woman crouched in front of her and gave her a good examination, up and down. "You look all right," she said. "I'm Clara. Who are you?"

"Kez," said Kez, looking around the fridge in a calculating sort of way. There were at least two ways out of the fridge that she could see—four if you counted the ways that only Kez could escape. "'Ow come you lot are still in 'ere, ay?"

"Because the ones that escaped all ended up in the freezer instead," muttered someone, and was hastily shushed.

That, Kez supposed, was fair enough. There were a few too many people in this fridge to escape without being noticed, and she had seen the weapons the kidnappers had: no one would want to risk running if they were only going to be shot for their trouble.

She turned her attention back on Clara and asked, "You lot been takin' sporks outta the tuckboxes?"

The woman looked at her for some time, thoughtfully, before she said, "No. That's them. They've been separating the sporks from the tuckboxes since they got here. The shipments are still going out, but nothing gets a spork."

"Figgered," said Kez, scowling. "Flamin' mongrels pinched everyone's sporks!"

"You'll have to be careful with that expression," Clara told her. She had green eyes that looked like they might usually be quite full of life, but right now they were full of warning. "They're not kind to people who look at them the wrong way. Come over with the others, kid."

"Told ya," Kez said. "Ain't cold."

"That isn't what I meant," Clara said patiently. "I meant that you should try to stay behind us bigger ones: it's a bit safer."

Kez stared at her for a while, then said to the huddle in general, "Orright, you lot 'ang out 'ere for a while, then. Got summink to do."

Clara said, more gently than before, "I don't think you understand, little one. You can't go out there: even if you did get out, they'd just shoot you and put you in the freezer."

"You can't tell a kid it'll be shot!" said one of the men, indignantly. "It's too young!"

"I'd rather she know than get shot," said Clara grimly. "If she's not too young to be shot, she's not too young to know the danger."

Kez gently kicked her leg, and when the woman looked down, grinned up at her. "You're nice," she said. "I'll make sure they let you out first, orright?"

Clara smiled as if she couldn't quite help it, her green eyes crinkling at the edges, and Kez took herself out of the fridge, but not out of time, and slipped away sideways to elsewhere in the production plant. Happily for her, she found herself in a room that had not only piles and piles of tuckboxes, but also two Seventh Worlders. They were busy packing white recon-plastic sporks into boxes, while the spork-less tuckboxes mounted up next to them.

When there were too many tuckboxes, one of them lifted the stack, grunting, and carried it away to the other end of the packing room and started throwing them in boxes there, still as spork-less as ever.

Kez pocketed one of the sporks from the nearest box, then wandered over to the closest of the two men and gave him a good kick to the back of the knee. He went over like a tree, backwards, and Kez gave the fleshy part of his upper arm a savage kick for good measure.

"That'll teach ya to steal me spork!" she said, as a pair of glazed eyes stared up at her.

She slipped sideways again, this time right into the Other Zone, and entered the timestream again in a different part of the plant just a minute or two earlier than she had left it. It took a little longer to find people, but Kez followed her ears until she found a group of four mixed Seventh and Fifth Worlders who were over by a vat of something pasty white and sludgy.

None of them saw her approach, and Kez didn't approve of being ignored: she picked up two abandoned tuckboxes and hurled them in the general direction of the vat. One struck the most unfortunate of the bunch on the back of the head, dropping him instantly, but the other sailed gloriously high and fast, and plopped down into the vanilla sludge with a satisfying *gloop*.

The other three men turned to face her attack as Kez slipped backward in time and a little bit sideways for the second time, and let herself come out in the considerably smaller fridge in the lunch room. To her great glee, she only had to wait a few seconds before someone pulled the door open, screamed, and slammed it shut again.

While that someone was still fumbling at the door to reef it open again, she shifted straight back into the walk-in fridge with the others, chuckling happily to herself.

"The *actual heck?*" said Clara blankly, staring at Kez. "How did you—what did you—do you have a *personal transporter?*"

"Incomin'!" Kez said happily.

"What?"

Hearing a growing babble of conflicting voices outside the fridge, Kez grinned and repeated, "Incomin'!"

"You'd better get behind me," said Clara, grabbing her collar with all the speed and efficiency of Marx. "They're not going to be happy if you've been stirring up trouble."

The babble grew until the lock rattled outside, and the door was wrenched open. Kez resisted the last, desperate tug that Clara made on her collar, and grinned at the trio of men, headed by Carrigan, who appeared in the doorway to stare at the group in the fridge for some time.

"You wouldn't be playing silly beggars, would you?" he said eventually, his eyes narrowed and as hard as stone.

"Wot you talkin' 'bout?" asked Kez. "Bin standin' 'ere wiv this lot."

Carrigan grabbed her out of Clara's grasp and went through her pockets with the professional thoroughness of a school-teacher who has been pranked one too many times. He found the plastic explosive and half a doughnut that had been there since last night, but Kez wasn't particularly worried about that. She knew where Marx kept the rest of the plastic explosive, after all, even if he didn't know she knew.

Carrigan tossed her back toward Clara, empty-handed, just as there was a wail in the distance. By Kez's best guess, something had happened that she had not yet done, and she was *very much* looking forward to finding out what that was.

"It's that dratted kid again!" howled someone outside the fridge.

Carrigan gave Kez one last glare, then slammed the door shut again. The lock chattered, and Kez immediately shifted out of the fridge and toward the sound of the voice she'd heard, jumping back by thirty seconds. She wanted the timing to be perfect.

It didn't take much time to find her next mark: Kez found herself in a secondary mixing room that looked as though it was waste management for all the offscourings of whatever white sludge was in the first one. It didn't occur to her to wonder if those potential offscourings were dangerous or not: she saw the man who was poised temptingly over the side of one of those vats just as he saw her. It was the one who had pinched her by the ear, and she took great glee in slipping across the room faster than he could react, to shove him into the vat.

With a wail, he caught at the assembly of filtration pipes that were above the vat, and Kez, very loudly this time, heard him yell, "It's that dratted kid again!"

Kez grinned and said, "Slippery, ain't they?" as she nodded at the pipes.

She heard his final wail as he lost his grip, but the splash was lost in her final shift back to the walk-in fridge. Kez, breathless with delight and laughter, nearly forgot to time her jump back into the fridge backward by a few seconds. She remembered at the last moment, which was just as well: the rattling of the lock was still going when the door abruptly opened once more and Carrigan's hard gaze swept the fridge's interior.

He hadn't completely locked the door, just as Kez had known he wouldn't. He had already checked her pockets and knew that she had no transporter, and he had seen her with his own eyes while someone was cursing her, but he wanted to be *sure*.

She smirked at him, and Carrigan strode back into the fridge. "You're coming with me, kid."

"Wait!" said Clara. "The kid didn't do anything—she's been standing here the whole time. How could she have done anything?"

Carrigan eyed her coldly. "I don't know," he said. "But she's coming with me."

He grabbed Kez by the ear, and Kez said cheerfully to Clara, "See ya later!" and trotted along with him, happy to see what would happen now that she was out of the fridge.

It was about time Marx did something, she thought. He should be thinking about how to rescue her by now—maybe he was trying to rescue everyone. He did things like that.

"Into the lunch room with you," Carrigan said, shoving her ahead of him. To the others, he said, "Lock the door again and check on Tony. Check on the stock, too: I don't like the way today's going."

Kez, who had decided that as much fun as she had been having, it was time to clear out and leave the plant to anyone who wanted to take it, wandered into the lunch room again and waited cheerfully for Carrigan. It wouldn't be hard to transport all the imprisoned staff out of harm's way, but Kez wasn't exactly sure how to best hurt the highly disagreeable men who were still in the plant.

That, she considered, was Marx's job. He was the one who always took care of people when he should run for his life, but he was also the one who made sure that the people hurting other people got a good kick in the face.

Kez was still wistfully thinking about kicking Carrigan in the face when that face itself appeared before her once again. It was, of course, attached to the body of Carrigan, which was too tall by a significant margin to make her dream any more than a wistful flutter in the back of her mind as he entered the lunch room and shut the door behind him.

"What," he said, with an entirely unconvincing pleasantness, "are we going to do with you?"

"Told ya before," said Kez, willing to explain. "Let them people outta the fridge."

"That's not going to happen," said Carrigan. "I don't know how you did it, but without the kind of personal transporters that my team have—that are, incidentally, *very expensive*—you've managed to be in three or four places at once. You've bitten, shoved into vats, knocked out, and terrorised my men, and neither you nor the workers are going anywhere until I figure out how you did it."

"Shows wot you know," muttered Kez. Marx was *very late*. He should have turned up to hit someone by now. She liked seeing him hit people in general, and she would very much like to see him hit this person in particular.

"I don't have any objections to hurting children, you know," he said. He jerked his chin toward the door and said, "Two of the bodies in the freezer are kids."

"Rubbish," said Kez. "'S'if they'd let kiddies into a production line!"

"They don't," Carrigan said, with a cold, sharp-edged smile. "But one of the more...troublesome staff members had two of her children doing schoolwork here in the lunch room."

"Don't like you," announced Kez. She saw herself reflected in his eyes, face pinched, eyes glittery and fathomless. "Fort you was just a pain in the neck but now I reckon we gotta do summink about you."

"And *what*," said Carrigan, through his teeth, reaching out to pinch her ear very tightly and painfully, "are you going to do about me?"

Kez didn't remember digging a hand into her pocket for the spork: it was just there with her hand wrapped around it, and she was looking down at it through hot, angry eyes. Carrigan saw it too, and he laughed.

She drove it straight into his leg, aiming for the soft inner thigh, and Carrigan half gasped, half screamed. Something warm trickled along Kez's fist when she pulled it away, and only half of the spork came with her, dripping with her blood and Carrigan's.

"Oi!" she said in surprise, staring at it. "It broke! Wot cheap rubbish is this?"

Carrigan gathered himself, gasping, and said with dark, venomous eyes, "Try to stab me again, and you'll be wondering about more than the sporks around here!"

"No, she's got a point," said Marx's voice from behind him, to Kez's glee.

Carrigan spun around just in time to receive a short, sharp jab to the face from Marx, who didn't believe in the gentlemanly habit of waiting for the other party to be ready. As Carrigan staggered back, blood dripping between the fingers clasping his nose, Marx stepped past him and removed the haft of the spork from Kez's fingers in one movement.

He looked down at the bloody plastic and added, "A sharp one, too."

"Yeah," said Kez resentfully, wiping her bloodied hand on his shirt, "but it ain't much good, is it? Broke right away!"

"I know, kid. That's the point you missed while you were busy stabbing people." Marx gestured chidingly at Carrigan with the remains of the spork. "This is garbage. What've you put in here to change the strength of the recon-plastic so badly?"

Kez understood at once. "Oi!" she said indignantly to Carrigan. "'Oo told you lollymen you could come in 'ere and mess wiv me food!"

The man glared at her as he wiped the blood from his face. "Nobody cares about your meal, you feral. And you're not going to be able to *prove* anything, either."

That last sentence was spat in Marx's direction.

"Don't reckon we'll have to prove anything," said Marx. "You've got about fifteen dead bodies in the freezer, and the most rudimentary testing will probably show that you've been smuggling out drugs in the form of recon-plastic sporks."

"By the time the WAOF get here, there'll be nothing much left of any of it except bodies and a very large explosion. If you don't think we're smart enough to have an exit strategy, you've got another think coming."

"Good luck putting it into action in the..." Marx checked the time "...sixty seconds you've got before they arrive."

Kez gave a delighted chuckle as Carrigan said blankly, "What?"

"Oh, and it won't just be the WAOF, it'll be Time Corp as well."

"*What?*"

Carrigan's comm screamed, "Boss! Boss, *incoming!*"

"WAOF or Time Corp?" he asked sharply.

"Both!"

His eyes narrow and furious, Carrigan snarled into his comm, "Use the portable shifters; get out what you can get out."

"About that," said Marx.

Kez hugged herself in glee. This was what she had been waiting for: glorious chaos.

"The portable shifters are the newest models, right? Nice pretty little things with red stripes and a few holes in the back?"

Carrigan went ashy grey and bawled into his communicator as if by the sheer volume of his voice he could prevent what had already happened. "*Stop!* Don't use the portable shifters! Do you hear me? *Don't use the portable shifters!*"

Mikkel heard the deeply satisfying tri-tone of the Core dropping a final result into the system just a moment before his lieutenant said exultantly, "Sir! We've got it! Deep space complex surround array; a small production plant attached to another factory. We're locked on!"

"Take her in," said Mikkel. "As quickly as you can."

"Isn't this fun, sir," said Arabella sunnily. "We're one of the most up-to-date and efficient ships in the known universe, and it'll still take sixty whole seconds to make all the calculations, lock on, and shift in and out."

"The known universe would be a lot safer if certain other people took as long," said Mikkel sourly. He was aware that his heart would be beating too quickly for the entirety of those sixty seconds, itching to be *in* and *doing*—until it was obvious that there was no longer even the slightest chance of catching Kez and Marx.

He was stubborn enough to want to catch them for the sake of having done it, while at the same time not quite convinced enough that they deserved imprisonment by the Time Corp to make the thought an entirely happy one. The day he actually caught them would be a day of mixed feelings.

But until that day arrived, Mikkel would do his best to obey his orders.

"Arrival in one RMU," called the lieutenant. "Emergency docking protocols are engaged and we should be able to be on board within thirty seconds of docking."

"Do they know we're coming?"

"Not unless they're tracking us, sir."

"WAOF on the line, sir!"

Mikkel looked blankly at his commander. "*WAOF*? Why?"

"I think they want us to stand down, sir. Something about lollymen and a known operation that they're pretty desperate to wriggle into."

"Put them through," Mikkel said, rather grimly. There was absolutely no way Time Corp would pull back for something so small as an operation of lollymen, even if they were associated with Uncle Cheng himself.

He turned away from his men for a modicum of privacy and said crisply, "Captain speaking. Go ahead."

"Liaison, sir. I know we've got an ETA of one RMU, so I'll be brief: we're not asking that you pull back. We want you to leave the lollymen to us, is all. We're pulling them onboard right now so we can go after the leader. Whoever else is left is all yours— barring any witnesses, of course."

"Have them out in the next thirty seconds," Mikkel said curtly. "We're slapping a time lock on the place after that, whether or not you're finished."

"Yes, sir. Thank you sir!"

The line went dead, and Mikkel said to his officers, "Time lock in twenty seconds, countdown starting...*now*."

. . .

There was only silence across the room; Carrigan looked around wildly and tapped his communicator, but Kez could tell from the lack of the normal, clicky pickup that no one was left on the channel.

"Lookit that!" she said. "Them expensive liddle transporters worked! Ain't you glad: they ain't broke!"

"Why aren't my men on the channel?" he demanded.

"Funny thing about that," said Marx, grinning humourlessly at the man. "The WAOF don't like prisoners running round with active communication devices. Particularly not communication devices that have been tapping their systems and might be used to warn off other conspirators."

"Did you—" Carrigan stopped, licking his top lip, and tried again. "What did you do?"

"You really shouldn't leave portable shifters around where anyone can play with them," Marx advised him. "Next time, you'll know to keep your gear all together with the prisoners so that you can keep an eye on it all."

"If I did that, the prisoners could—I'm not taking advice from a thief!"

"You got a bad attitude," Kez told him.

"*I've* got—you *bit* my enforcer."

Marx raised his brows. "You might need a new enforcer, in that case. Don't know how you're going to pay one, now that the WAOF is about to seize all your assets, but I'm sure you can find one cut-price. He might be a bit smaller than your last one, that's all."

"An' that's *after* you get outta the brig," Kez said, with something of a malicious glee in her voice. "Reckon everyone's gunna be pretty interested in speakin' wiv you lot."

"I don't know why you're so pleased with yourself," Carrigan said venomously. "If I can't get out, neither can you; and I'm betting you're wanted by the Time Corp yourself. I'd be surprised if the WAOF aren't after you, too."

"Why else d'you reckon Time Corp are 'ere?" Kez scoffed. "'*Course* they're after us!"

"Then how do you expect to get out of this without being caught? If you think you're going to get away with sixty seconds' lead time—"

"Ten."

"What?"

"Ten," said Kez, louder. "You already spent fifty seconds chunterin'."

He stared at her in speechless rage, and eventually said, "You're both lying. No way you'd call WAOF and Time Corp down on yourself if you didn't have enough time to get away, too."

"You already forgotten the fun we 'ad this arvo? Time ain't a problem for us," Kez said; and, grabbing Marx by the hand, she shifted them both a little bit sideways and a little bit backwards until they were in the *Upsydaisy* five minutes ago by RMUs.

"Been busy, ain't ya?" Kez said in a congratulatory sort of way as Marx kicked the *Upsydaisy* into life and motion. "'Ow'd you get the idea for all o'that, then?"

"Let's just say that as much as pure, feral energy is your strength, guerrilla warfare is mine. I had a lot of time on my hands, and they weren't expecting someone to go through their things instead of leaving or calling the WAOF. They were listening to all stations anyway, so they would have heard a call and come to find me. I just closed a few doors and made sure no one could run away too quickly once the WAOF started paying attention to the very obvious tap on their system."

Kez grinned. "That's flamin' beautiful. Ain't no need to call the grey boys if they're already wonderin' why you're tappin' their system. Oi. Wot were ya gunna do to get me outta there?"

"Beggar all," said Marx, with devastating simplicity.

"Oi!" Kez said indignantly. "You were gunna leave me there? Fort you was figgerin' out what to do to rescue me!"

"You stepped into someone else's problem," Marx told her.

"*And* you could have stepped out of it at any moment by shifting. I was here strictly as backup. Besides, I wanted to know what they were up to, and you were distracting them very nicely."

"Rude!" said Kez, but she grinned. With a warm contentment in her chest, she said, "Did all right, didn't I?"

"Exactly the right amount of feral," agreed Marx. "Thought you were going to have that poor bloke's hand off for a moment or two."

"Couldn't 'elp it!" protested Kez. She thought about it, and explained, "Usually I'm more careful, see? Don't wanna be swallowin' some mucker's blood. Was just tryin' to hold on for dear life—'e wasn't 'arf strong!"

"Yes, I saw you go flying," said Marx. "That was a nice bit of work. Have you been practising your shifts?"

Kez grinned. "Well. S'pose I been doin' summink like that. You said I shouldn't be showin' so many people wot I can do, so I figgered it was a good way av doin' it."

"Well done, kid."

"Oi!" said Kez, belatedly remembering something. "Wot time is it? Local time, I mean; when we went to the production plant? 'Cos I can't remember if Uncle Cheng 'as met us yet, and maybe we oughtta been more careful 'bout shiftin' in front av that bloke."

"We should have been more careful about not storming production plants in search of plastic sporks," said Marx. "But here we are! Listen, kid; it's no good crying over flaming fuel. There's nothing we can do about it now."

"'T'least we know how he got a handle on us," Kez said, scowling darkly. "Been wonderin' about that. Reckon that bloke must escape or summink—later on, like."

"Or be bailed out," Marx said, nodding. "It depends on how well connected he is. If he is connected to Uncle Cheng, he'll be out soon; out, and telling his boss about us."

"Well, we already thumbed our noses at 'im," said Kez. "So that's—'ang on. *'Ang* on."

Marx's hard grey eyes met her black ones. He nodded slowly. "The Core's a mess lately, and Uncle Cheng reckoned he'd be after us. He has the money and the network to make the kind of trouble we've been running into lately."

"Yeah," Kez said grimly, "but 'e ain't got the expertise wiv time—not when it comes to us. Reckon Marcus is back, Marx."

She hoped he'd deny it again: he always did when she brought up that particular fear. Deny it, or say that he'd killed him and there was no way Marcus could claw his way back to life.

But this time, Marx said, "Yeah, maybe, kid."

"You said 'e wasn't comin' back," she said, her voice snubby.

"Yep," said Marx, his voice as tough as the leathery skin of his face. "But if he's stupid enough to come back, I'll just kill him again."

"Shoulda worked the first time," Kez said. "Shouldn't 'ave to do it again. Uncle Cheng shouldn't be stoppin' people wot are supposed to die from dyin'."

Marx frowned. "If he did decide to use Solomon, he hasn't changed the fact of Marcus' death—not yet, at any rate. We would have been able to see that in the Core."

"Yeah, reckon he knew we'd be able to see that. Reckon he got hold of Marcus when 'e was younger." Kez thought about that and added, "Reckon 'e would have promised to help Marcus get out of dyin' if Marcus would give 'im some inside info on 'ow to get us, see?"

"I see. Time for us to be digging back into the Core, I think."

Kez grinned her delight. "Right! I'll go get TuanTuan, then, eh?"

"No one said anything about your little toy friend," Marx objected.

"Did so too!"

"Listen, kid; do you think I'm not capable of poking around in the Core on my own?"

"Nah, but TuanTuan's *scary* good!" said Kez, still happy. "Let's kidnap 'im, Marx! 'E'll like a nice, luverly holiday, won't 'e?"

She found that Marx was gazing at her in something like fascination. He said, "Well, I suppose you know best about that, but I'm not sure where you get that idea from. Last time you kidnapped him he was dangling by the leg from our hold and screaming for help."

Kez made a small *pft!* noise. "Wot rubbish: 'e was 'aving a lark. Anyway, if we're goin' ta be messin' wiv the Core again, he's the one wot does all the maths, so I reckon we should kidnap 'im."

Marx looked at her for a moment or two, then said with terrifying accuracy, "He's safe, you know. They might suspect a connection between him and us, but there isn't a trace of direct contact between us yet that isn't marked as accidental in the Core. Tuan isn't going to be in danger if we don't go and fetch him right now, this minute."

Kez hugged her arms around herself and said in a gruff voice, "Dunno wot yore on about. TuanTuan's the one wot knows about this stuff. We gotta go get 'im."

"Kid, he's safe. There's no connection between us big enough to be noticed: if we keep going to see him, there will be."

"They might not know about him 'zactly," Kez said, "but Marcus is scary good at makin' connections, and, and—anyway, I'm goin' to see TuanTuan. You can do wot you want."

"All right, all right, kid," said Marx, grabbing the back of her jumper. "No need to get huffy. We might as well kidnap someone's heir: what else have we got to do today?"

Kez obeyed the tug on her jumper, though she could have shifted away and they both knew it. Marx grinned the tough, dry grin at her that she liked, and, pushing things, she asked, "Can I fly the *Upsydaisy* on the way, then?"

"Oh, why not," said Marx. "Might as well give my heart a good workout while we're at it. You go ploughing into any more goat sheds and I'll leave you in one, though."

DRUGS ON TAP

"No, I *swear*; we got a group of Uncle Cheng's lollymen this morning!" insisted the constable. Her face was flushed with a combination of the mess hall's Third World curry and righteous indignation. "I was in the comms room this morning when everything went down; I'm the one who found the ring!"

"Bet you got a tip through the comms and just don't want to admit it," said someone. "Uncle Cheng doesn't just give up his men like that: no one catches them."

The constable glared at that someone. "Well, I did! And I didn't *have* to follow a tip—the idiots tipped us off themselves! It was the second tap they started on our comms that gave them away: if we hadn't seen it, they'd still be running drugs across the Twelve Worlds."

Reprovingly, a detective said, "No one would be that stupid. They already had a tap on our system comms: they knew everything we were up to, *and* I know for a fact that no one detected it, because I was with the internal boys who found it afterward. They'd apparently been tapping us for the last few months."

"I know!" she said. "But they started a second one up!"

"They'd *have* to know we'd be more likely to notice them if they did that!" protested a bright young sergeant. "Who'd put on a second tap when they already know what we're doing?"

"That's not all," the constable said. "They used a *second gen* tap. One of the old ones that makes its own channel and gives double-ended access."

There was a chorus of scoffing around the room. One of the other female constables said, "If lollymen went around doing that sort of thing, any of us could be up for a promotion next! We could just wait around in the comms room!"

"You read the AAR," the first constable said to her partner. "There were two taps mentioned, weren't there? *Weren't there?*"

All eyes fell on her partner, who ducked his head and said, "There were two mentioned."

"That wasn't all," the constable said, with quiet triumph. The others already didn't believe her; they definitely wouldn't believe what she was about to say next. That was all right: she had a prominent place in the AAR, and she was quite sure she was looking at an early promotion, which was no doubt why her partner was so out of sorts. "They gave the channel a name."

Disbelieving laughter erupted all around the room.

"They gave the *tap* a *name?*"

"What'd they call it? *Come and get us, we're idiots?*"

"Close," she said, and despite everything, she couldn't help grinning. "They named it *We've got drugs. Come get us. We double dare you.*"

*HOW TO MAKE FIRES AND IMMOLATE
PEOPLE*

ARABELLA HAD NEVER PARTICULARLY CARED FOR GARDENING; she hadn't ever been able to keep a plant alive for more than a few weeks since childhood, although she was conscientious about watering and appropriate amounts of the appropriate kinds of light. She had come to the conclusion that plants didn't care to live with her and, given their unfortunate and rather depressing tendency to commit herbal suicide rather than remain with her, had given up trying.

Gardening in the Facility was something different. The Facility itself was different from the Fourth World Orbiting WAOF station where Arabella had hitherto lived most of her life, and she had spent several minutes that morning just trying to get out of her room until she found the right button to press. The rooms and corridors didn't have the same feeling that the specifically calibrated gravity on the Orbiting station gave, either, though Arabella wasn't sure whether that was a bad or a good thing.

The gardening, though; that was the biggest difference. Arabella was rather certain that this difference sprang from the green-haired Eighth Worlder who had been given his own glass-covered dome for gardening in the Facility's vast courtyard. Arabella didn't know his name, but he must have been important, because not only was he given his own quadrant, but nobody objected when he began growing one of the most virulent and actively venomous strains of Fourth World poison ivy within a dome that would have been protective if it wasn't supposed to be containing Fourth World poison ivy.

Fifteen-year-old Arabella, fresh from an orbiting station that had only had unpleasantly damp hydroponics bays, had spent most of her free mornings in the courtyard gardens, aware that she had only a certain amount of free time left. Soon, she would start her training, and then free time would be strictly limited. Arabella wasn't entirely sure why she had been chosen by the Facility out of thousands of applicants, but she knew she would need to work hard to prove herself the correct choice. She hadn't been the brightest in her classes, and she certainly hadn't been the most obedient or civic-minded, either—in fact her Ethics in Law teacher had begun to develop a noticeable twitch, and the Freedom of Information and Ethics of Concealment sub-teacher wasn't far behind him.

Arabella wasn't even sure she *was* the correct choice, if it came to that.

Still, she was happy to be at the Facility. She had been orphaned early, and had seen enough of the world on her Fourth World Orbiting station to know that the authorities weren't always necessarily right merely because they were in authority. She was also a great believer in understanding the enemy, so to speak, and although authority weren't necessarily always the enemy, they always had the promise to become so.

Training under Time Corp or WAOF, but *particularly* at the Facility, should see her able to get a job anywhere in the known universe—or, if something went terribly wrong, to be able to avoid either group as much as possible.

So, with two days of freedom remaining to her, Arabella decided to familiarise herself with the two floors she had yet to explore before returning to the courtyard for a nice afternoon stroll. She went first to the library floor, which, in keeping with its archaic name, held real books as well as consoles with access to every other writing known to the Twelve Worlds. Unlike the WAOF station she'd come from, the corridors and rooms were carpeted, which made browsing between the rooms a rather ghostly affair. Arabella couldn't hear her own footsteps, let alone those of anyone else, and she was frequently startled by the sudden appearance of other trainees or staff members around a corner.

When she tired of startling at unexpected people, Arabella abandoned the library floor and took the stairs to the next level down, wandering silently along carpeted corridors until she rounded a corner to see an odd pair of strangers ahead of her.

Neither of the strangers were particularly tall, but the robes they wore made them seem significantly shorter and squatter. Arabella wondered at the robes until she caught sight of the computerised speech system protruding from the side of the hooded helmet of each: usually such robes and systems were used by burn victims whose skin and vocal cords had been damaged beyond repair or speech.

What two burn victims were doing at the Facility, she didn't know. What she did know was that they were lacking the red Facility tag that all visitors should have, along with the lanyard that staff or trainees would have.

Curious, Arabella followed them. Technically, she couldn't be disciplined for not turning in strange visitors when she hadn't been instructed to catch them or warn about them, or even begun her training. She was just a pre-trainee. She didn't know better. She hadn't been trained.

She was still smiling to herself when the two robed visitors turned into one of the briefing rooms. Arabella stole in quickly and silently behind them, passing behind the giant briefing screen by the door while they were fussing with the controls for the same, and ducked behind a few rows of extra chairs.

One of them said in voice that came robotically through its speaker function, "How does this thing work?"

"Just plug it in," said the other, just as mechanically. "He said that would work."

"He should have come with us, then. I prefer pinching evidence to planting it."

"We're not planting evidence, we're just putting real evidence where the right people can see it."

"Yeah, but I don't—heck, here they come!"

There was a ruffling of material, and the two robed figures, who had been just slightly visible between the chairs, dived for cover behind the stacks on the other side of the room. Arabella wriggled a little further between serried lines of seats and tucked herself into the rounded bowl of a chair at the top of one of the shorter stacks, well out of sight. If she was caught anywhere she shouldn't be at the Facility, Arabella would be subject to forced recalibration. The doctors tried their best to remove only those memories that people shouldn't have, but it was a process liable to small mistakes— which small mistakes quite often ended in significantly larger problems later on.

She wasn't particularly interested in the briefing, which had something to do with a couple of aberrations that were currently making crimps in the universe, but midway through the process, Arabella was quite certain she heard the name Gormley mentioned once. That made her pop her head up just in time to catch sight of what seemed to be surveillance footage from a Time Corp sloop displaying on the screen.

In it, a small child drove something that looked like a screwdriver into the leg of a tall, golden-haired man who was dressed in the uniform of a Time Corp captain. The gathered people around the room collectively drew in a sympathetic breath, muffling Arabella's own hiss of sympathy.

Arabella, who was very familiar with the casual violence of WAOF and Time Corp officers, expected to see the captain back-hand the child across the room, but he didn't. Instead, he wrenched the object out of his leg, seemed to take a moment to recover himself, and spoke to the child. As he did, she saw his eyes—patient and kind and very blue—and felt a tickle of interest. She knew only one other officer with kind eyes, Sergeant Gormley of the orbiting station, and his eyes had never been so bewilderingly beautiful. They were merely kind and likeable.

Arabella didn't like to be bewildered, so she sank back down in her seat, and allowed the babble of discussion to fill the air around her. By the time it occurred to her to pay attention again so that she could learn who the captain was, the briefing had moved on. She gazed at the ceiling instead, waiting until the briefing was over and the crowd moved out, prompting the lights to flicker off once again; then again while the other two interlopers would likely be trying to leave without being seen.

She had begun to wonder, distantly, if all of this was a test for her first week. Was she expected to do something?

While she thought about that, Arabella heard the two remaining people shuffling around in their slightly-too-big robes, but instead of moving toward the door, they edged toward her.

They were coming right to her chair. They knew she was there.

For once thankful for the fact that she was most often still taken for twelve years old instead of fifteen, Arabella at once curled herself up, draped one arm artfully over the seat of the chair and, tucking her head into the roundness of the chairback, pretended to be asleep.

She was able to hold the pretence until she felt a hovering presence that must be someone hanging over the stacks of chairs and a voice said conversationally, "I know you're not asleep—saw you come in after us."

"Bother!" said Arabella, sitting up at once. "Why didn't you say something, then?"

The robed figure leaning casually on the stack of chairs closest shrugged. "Looked like you were having fun. First time at the Facility?"

"Yes," Arabella said, climbing over the seats in front of her so that she didn't have to pass too close to the taller figure. She wanted to be able to run for it if necessary.

The shorter figure wriggled off the seat it had been perching on to peer at her. "Us too. Maybe. Who knows, at this point?"

"Shouldn't you know if you've already been somewhere?" asked Arabella.

"Should," said the taller one. "But the universe is temporarily a bit unstable, so half the time we don't know if we're coming or going."

"Is this a test?"

"No," said the smaller one.

"Maybe," said the taller one. "Anyway, we'd better get going before the alarms go off."

"Too late," Arabella told them. She had already seen the delicate pulsing of light running along the skirting boards—green for *intruders detected*. She pointed at it. "They know someone's here."

"Probably not us," argued the smaller figure.

"Probably not," said the other. "But do we want to stay and find out?"

"Yeah, I suppose not." A hand came out of the robes, roughened by age but surprisingly unblemished despite the burn robes, and the smallest figure tossed a small storage chip at Arabella. "Got a copy of that footage if you want it."

Arabella caught it, and asked, "Why are you giving this to me?"

"Looked like you might want it," explained the figure. "Saw your head peeping up."

"Who is he? The captain who got stabbed in the leg?"

The taller of the figures made a small chirrup of noise that might have been an electronic laugh. "Trouble," it said. "You should probably stay away."

"He has nice eyes," said Arabella. "Why did that little girl stab him?"

"Probably had a reason," the smaller figure said. "He's a nice bloke, though. He's going to need some help if he wants to stay alive."

"He's featured a lot in the Core," said the taller, in a meditative sort of way. "A person could get a lot of information there, just for starters."

"C'mmon," said the other. "That light's giving me the willies."

"How are you going to get away?" asked Arabella, fascinated. "Personal transporters and time travel are both things that this system will catch."

The taller robed figure seemed to stare at her for a while before it said, "You're pretty small to know the sort of things you know."

"I'm small for my age," said Arabella. "I think you're confusing intelligence with height."

"Knew I was doing something wrong."

"That's the thing," said the shorter of the two, its robotic voice somehow smug. "People can only put in security for stuff they know about. The other stuff—well, they don't know what they don't know, see?"

"They're pretty quick at learning, though," Arabella pointed out. "And there's a person here working on the new security system for Eighth World who makes really good guesses."

"You aren't supposed to be helping us get away," said the taller. "Anyone might think we're friendly with you."

"I saw you adding information to the debrief package," explained Arabella. "And I'm still not sure that you're not a test. I might not be supposed to be helping you, but I'm pretty sure you're engaged in a bit of guerrilla helping, yourself."

"Good point," said the shorter. It seemed to stare at her for a while, then unexpectedly asked, "What are you doing here? At the Facility, I mean. We didn't expect to see you here."

"I don't know, myself," Arabella said, absolutely truthfully. "But I'm jolly well going to take advantage of my time here, I can tell you."

"Good girl," the taller said, its robotic voice oddly approving.

Arabella tried not to feel too warm at the approval. There were a lot of forms of manipulation, but manipulation by approval was one she particularly hated, and she didn't want to leave herself open to it.

"Well, if you aren't going to make a noise or run for it, we'd better be off," said the shortest one, opening the storage cupboard. It poked the larger figure in the region of the ribs, making Arabella wince, and both of them shuffled into the space.

"Wait!" protested Arabella. "That's the storage cupboard!"

Ignoring her, they shut the door behind them, and she heard a brief, violent surge of noise before there was utter silence. Arabella shut her mouth and collected herself enough to put the storage chip into her pocket, but when she approached the cupboard and opened it, it was empty.

Wondering if she would have to explore the entire Facility for signs of secret passages or hidden transporters, Arabella thoughtfully took herself outside and downstairs into the court-yard gardens.

They were empty, which was slightly disappointing, but she would still be able to go to her favourite part of the gardens—the glass-domed poison-ivy garden—even if she couldn't talk to its owner. Arabella liked to look at it and wonder who would be brave enough to go in there and garden: it was set out in a circle, with spokes of poison-ivy making a wagon-wheel with the main clump in the centre. That clump in the centre, Arabella knew, was the hive mind of the plant. Everything the poison-ivy spokes took in by way of nourishment and nutrient, would be sent to the hive mind at the centre. If an unwary human were to step into the dome, the hive mind would also send out tendrils to smother and overcome it.

It was a garden, in fact, that was a contradiction in terms. No one could garden it without dying, and any attempt to stop the ivy spreading beyond its original pattern would fail—as would any attempts to kill it.

Arabella had been curious about it since she arrived, and owed her current level of knowledge about that particular strain of poison-ivy to her acquaintance with the owner of the garden; that green-haired Eighth Worlder who never seemed to speak to anyone else.

If she was at first disappointed not to meet him in the garden, when she got closer to the garden with the odd sensation of heat teasing her through the hedges, Arabella caught sight of a familiar sprout of hair standing out against a glassy dome.

Normally his hair wouldn't stand out against the greenery, but today, the garden beneath the dome seemed to be on fire. Not all of it; merely some parts of it.

"Hallo!" said Arabella, childishly glad to see him. Other

walkers in the garden tended to avoid him and this area in general, but Arabella was fond of both of them. "Did you decide you don't want the trouble of gardening after all?"

He looked across at her, a faint frown between his brows. "I am gardening."

"Oh." Arabella came to a stop beside him, and observed the spot fires that had been lit where each spoke of poison ivy met the edges of the garden. "This is gardening?"

"Yes."

Arabella gazed at it for a moment longer, and said, "That's right. It's not killable, is it? So the fire won't hurt it."

She still didn't see how that could be considered gardening, but if it couldn't kill the ivy...

"It's almost unkillable," corrected the green-haired man. "Everything that tries to kill it gets killed before it can kill the plant. That's what the hive mind does. Fire itself can't kill the plant, so it doesn't see it as a threat."

"So it's...not going to kill the plant?"

"No, it's going to kill it."

Arabella hadn't talked to him for three mornings without getting some sense of how to communicate with him. Plainly, she asked, "How?"

"It's a matter of lighting the fires in the right places," said the green-haired man, pointing a slender finger at the spot fires. "I told you: the fire itself doesn't kill the plant, so it doesn't try to fight against it. It just sends it up along to the hive mind, the same as everything else. But as soon as there's enough fire from enough sources, it starves the hive mind of oxygen and it dies. Once it dies, all the spokes of the wheel are separated and turn into discrete entities; you can grow it without worrying that it's going to take over the whole place due to the hive mind."

Arabella suggested, "Divide and conquer?"

"That's one part of it, but the point is—"

"To kill the hive mind before it knows it's being killed and can try to defend itself."

"Exactly," said the green-haired man. He didn't sound exactly congratulatory or even particularly impressed, but he seemed satisfied. "It's what we do here."

Arabella gazed at him in slight suspicion. In her experience, adults didn't tell kids stuff like this. "Are you supposed to be telling me this?"

The man shrugged. "You're one of the spokes, so I don't see why you shouldn't know."

"I'm what?"

"You're a spoke," he said. "One day, someone will come along and set fire to you, and before you know it, ten other spokes will be on fire. Everything will seem just fine because fire can't kill him, and he won't know he's dying of oxygen deprivation until he's dead. Then everything will separate again, and the Core won't know where the connections are to be able to stop it before it happens."

Arabella felt vaguely insulted. "Are you saying I'm poisonous?"

He peered down at her. "It's always a mistake to take analogies too far. Did I hurt your feelings? I forget to ask sometimes."

"No," said Arabella, after a few moments' thought. "Do you mean that you're trying to get something done and you're going at it through a lot of different channels?"

"No," he said.

He didn't say anything else, but Arabella had the impression that it wasn't because he had nothing else to say—like the door panel that morning, it was because she hadn't pressed the right buttons yet.

After a few moments of thought, she asked, "Do you mean someone else is trying to get something done through pyromaniac gardening?"

This time, he looked distinctly pleased. "That's a good question. Yes. They're setting things on fire in just the right place to bring about the right result. We're just piggy-backing on that to kill our own hive mind. Maybe we're just a spoke: usually we're the gardener, so everything feels a bit odd."

Arabella felt the warmth of the fire on her cheeks as the reflected glow of the flames danced across her face. Before her eyes, the central hive mind, or bush, or whatever it was, flamed with fire but didn't wither.

"It looks fine to me," she said. "When is it going to die?"

"That's because the plant itself is feeding on the fire right now," said the man. "It'll do that for a few hours before the lack of oxygen around the centre nest kills off the hive mind. Once the hive mind is dead and all the connections are lost, we'll be able to plant whatever we want in the segments. The spokes are still dangerous and poisonous to the touch, but they don't actively try to kill anyone or take over the space because they aren't being sent directives to do so."

"Why did you plant it, if it's so dangerous?"

"Because it's also very useful for keeping people away from things they shouldn't touch," he said. "And because it looks more dangerous than it is. And because some things should be kept separate from other things."

Arabella would have liked to tell him that none of that made any kind of objective sense, but something else occurred to her instead. "Just a minute," she said, alarmed. "Is someone trying to kill someone I know?"

He had said she was a spoke—had said someone was going to die.

"There you go again." He sounded gloomy. "Taking the analogy too far. Or not far enough, I suppose: your hive mind is quite a bit more self-aware than they usually are. It's trying to detach everything without dying—that's what happens when a hive mind tries to protect its branches instead of demanding food. The hive mind I'm talking about doesn't know it's in danger."

"Oh. Who is my hive mind?"

"You'll find out soon enough," he said.

"Well, what about this hive mind that you're working on?"

"It's very delicate," he said, his face lighting up. "I have to make sure I calculate everything just right; snatch a spork here, leak a confidential Institute record there, make a sure a certain hunter is hired instead of another—"

"So you *are* trying to kill someone," Arabella said, in gloomy certainty.

"Technically, yes, I suppose," said the other. "But that's not the *point*—well, I suppose it *is* the point, but it's not the first point. It's the final point. A Fixed Point, if we get it right."

"You're trying to make a Fixed Point out of someone's death? Isn't that against the WAOF and Time Corp charters? Deliberately making new Fixed Points?"

"We're not exactly WAOF or Time Corp, here," he said. "So we have different rules. You should know that."

"Does everyone else know that?"

"I hope not. That would make things very difficult."

"I'm rather certain you should be in jail," said Arabella. She was rather certain that most of the staff at the Facility ought to be in jail, but that was another matter in which her Ethics in Concealment teacher would never agree with her.

The man shot her a look and then went back to looking at the garden-on-fire. "That would be a waste."

He certainly shouldn't be telling her what he was telling her. Arabella wondered momentarily if he was just a crazy man, and that was why no one else talked with him, but she was aware that the Facility chose people for a reason. Crazy he might be, but he would be a useful sort of crazy.

"Why are you making a Fixed Point of someone's death?" she asked.

"Because they're the hive mind, of course. If we don't make a Fixed Point of it, someone might come back and get him out of it."

The sheer ruthlessness of it took her breath away. "Who are you going to kill?"

"I'm not going to tell you," he said, peering down at her again. "You're a spoke, but you're in someone else's hive mind *and* you're still a young one. You could go off and form a hive mind of your own if I'm not careful. We already have enough trouble."

"All right," said Arabella. "Then tell me this: who are you really working for?"

"I'm more of an off-shoot than a spoke," he told her. "And for your information, I *am* working for the Incursion Specialists here at the Facility."

"That's not all of it, though," she said, suspicious. She felt that she was very close to understanding why she had been brought to the Facility. "All right, fine. Don't tell me. I don't care."

"Yes, you do," he said accurately. "But I won't tell you anyway. You're too dangerous."

"If I'm too dangerous, I'm surprised you're telling me anything. I haven't even had my proper training yet."

"It was a course of action recently recommended to me," he explained. "I took into account all the variables and came to the conclusion that it was the best course."

"I suppose I should be flattered," Arabella said. 'Truthfully, she was. But she was also worried, and she wasn't sure which feeling she ought to be giving the most weight. Testingly, she asked, "Am I more or less likely to meet that captain now that I know this?"

He shouldn't have known what she was talking about, but she wasn't surprised to see him taking a moment to think about it— not as though he was trying to figure out what she was talking about, but as though he was busy doing the kind of computations that she had seen scrolling across one of the computers yesterday.

At last he blinked, and said, "How interesting. If my calculations are correct, far more likely."

"All right," said Arabella. "Then you don't have to tell me who you're really working for."

"I wasn't going to tell you."

"Do you know when it will die?" asked Arabella, tilting her chin at the garden.

"I've got a very good idea," he said.

"What about the other one? The hive mind that's a person?"

"Once everything is set up, I should know to within an hour or two, but I should think it will happen just about the time that you go on your honeymoon."

Arabella very nearly opened her mouth to ask him what on earth he meant by that, but managed to keep it shut for just long enough to think of a more important question.

"When's that, then?" she asked instead. "My honeymoon?"

"I like you!" he said approvingly. "You ask the right questions. You'll have to wait and see on that one: it's in flux, just like the rest of this lot at the moment. The fire is catching, but the hive mind isn't yet dead. And that reminds me—can you go to the toilet at exactly eleven hundred LRT today?"

"I don't know how it works on your world," said Arabella, "but I don't have my internal systems on that accurate of an internal clock."

He looked at her for a moment or two, as if trying to decide whether or not she was joking. "You don't have to relieve yourself," he explained. "Just sit in there. When someone knocks, tell him it's occupied."

Amused, Arabella asked, "Do you have a particular toilet in mind?"

"Of course. It would be ridiculous to ask you to sit in a toilet just anywhere in the Facility at eleven hundred LRT."

"Of course it would. Does this have something to do with the two robed people who are walking around inside?"

"Absolutely not," he said firmly. "In fact, I'm trying very hard to make sure that there is no connection whatsoever between them. We'll have a lot of trouble if there is."

"I suppose that's why it has to be eleven o'clock," suggested Arabella.

"Exactly."

They watched the fire in silence for a few moments, then the green-haired man looked down at her again as if surprised.

"Off you go, then," he said. "You can come back tomorrow for the death. You'll need to use the toilet on the personnel floor, fourth corridor. You can make it if you hurry."

With twenty RMUs to go until she apparently *needed* to be in a toilet on the personnel floor, Arabella should have been able to take her time without feeling particularly rushed. But there was a ticking pulse behind her ear urging her to hurry, urging her to get where she needed to go.

Perhaps that was the fault of the green-haired man—and why hadn't she gotten his name today, either? she wondered—or perhaps it was just that she suddenly felt a sense of purpose she'd been lacking, and didn't want to ruin the work she'd been given.

Or perhaps she just didn't want to miss out on improving her chances of meeting the captain with the kind eyes.

Arabella hurried along, content for now not to wonder too much which of the reasons was uppermost in her mind, and collided with two familiar figures as she entered the main building again and turned to take the corridor to the closest lift.

The taller one muttered something in Third World dialect that must have been a swear, even though Arabella first thought it was *eggs*! Since *eggs* didn't make sense, she let it go and merely said, "Sorry. Wasn't watching where I was going. How did you get out of the cupboard, by the way?"

"Where are you off to in a hurry?" asked the shorter of the two.

"I have to go to the toilet," she said, without blinking.

An accusing stare made itself felt from the depths of the hood of the shortest one. "That's suspicious."

"Very suspicious," said the taller. "Why are you suddenly off to the loo?"

"I'm fairly sure I'm not allowed to tell you," Arabella said. It was rather satisfying to say that to two mysterious figures who had been baiting her with their mysteriousness earlier.

The two figures seemed to look at each other. One shrugged; the other said, "Fair enough, I suppose."

Arabella's first instinct was to hurry along, but given that she had plenty of time, and the green-haired man had urged her to hurry, she wondered suddenly if this was what she had been hurrying for—one last chance to see the mysterious strangers before she went to play silly beggars in a toilet upstairs.

And she *very much* wondered if this was the doing of the Incursion Specialists themselves, or if they were being infiltrated.

"You're supposed to be out of here by eleven o'clock, aren't you?" she asked them.

"Good grief," said the taller of the two. "She knows a lot more than I was expecting her to know at this age. Irritating, isn't it?"

The smaller one stared at Arabella for a few moments before agreeing, "Flaming irritating. I don't like this. C'mmon, let's get out of here."

"I wanted to ask some more questions," Arabella protested. There were still about fifteen minutes to spare.

"Well, as you so succinctly put it, we're supposed to be out of here by eleven," said the taller one. "C'mmon, robot-breath."

The smaller figure back-handed him in the stomach. "Watch it, or I'll leave you behind," it said.

"Wait!" called Arabella, as they strode past her and toward the other end of the corridor. "But what were you here for?"

They stopped briefly and turned, and she had the feeling that if she could have seen the faces within the hoods, they would have been grinning.

The smaller of the two said, "Making fires," in its robotic voice.

"Immolating people," added the taller of the two. "We'll be seeing you. Might have a bit of work for you later."

"Wait!" Arabella said again, as they swept around the corner, but she was too late. By the time she darted around the corner, there was no one in the hall. Of the silence of the corridor, she asked, "Are you my hive mind, then?"

Nobody answered, but they didn't really have to: Arabella had already made up her own mind about that. She checked her time-piece and started for the lifts at the end of the corridor.

It was time to go to the toilet.

THE ART OF PYROMANIAC GARDENING: AN EXCERPT

"HAVE YOU SEEN THE NOTICEBOARD THIS MORNING, MY darling?"

Arabella wasn't surprised when Mikkel looked over the top of his coffee at her, suspicion in every line of his face.

"No," he said. "And I'm not going to, either. It's our honeymoon: I don't care what those two pains-in-my-rear-end are up to."

She sat down beside him on the rug and pushed the biscuits closer on the coffee-table. "What would you like to talk about instead?"

"I'd like to talk about the fact that I haven't had more than two kisses this morning, and that puts my daily average down from yesterday, which might have been an aberration but in my opinion should be made the new norm."

"I didn't like to interrupt your coffee-drinking," explained Arabella, tilting her head up a little to press a kiss into the warm skin just below his ear. "And I think you were going to ask me something last night before we got...carried away."

Mikkel grinned into his coffee like a schoolboy, but he said seriously enough, "You never told me how you came to work for your employers."

"It's a long story," said Arabella. She turned a prim smile on

Mikkel and explained, "And of course, there was the issue of incriminating myself. Now that we're married—"

"Anything that incriminates you also incriminates me," Mikkel finished. He sent her a reproachful look that very nearly had her believing its sincerity until he added, "I knew there was a reason you agreed to marry me."

"There were several reasons," Arabella told him, a laugh catching in her throat. "But that was certainly one of the unexpected side-benefits."

Mikkel raised a brow at her.

"Well, perhaps not unexpected," allowed Arabella. "But it was merely the cherry on top, I do assure you!"

"I'd certainly like to think so," said Mikkel affably. "If only for the sake of my poor, bruised ego! I am curious about one thing, however."

"Just one? That's very well-adjusted of you, my darling."

"In my optimism, I like to imagine we'll be able to get to everything else in a pleasingly leisurely manner," murmured Mikkel. "I like to imagine that we have many years ahead of us yet to get to know each other."

"I *could* give you a solid answer to that," Arabella said. "But then I'd have to kill you and that would be a pity, not to mention creating a self-destroying paradox, which is a no-no in my line of work."

"It's a no-no in anyone's line of work," Mikkel said. "And I don't think you could kill me at this point, anyway. I'm far too adorable. But leaving aside my adorableness and the many benefits of aligning yourself with me, what on earth could someone offer you as bait that would get you to wriggle yourself into the life and affairs of a Time Corp captain and otherwise duck around in time and space at their bidding?"

"I don't think you understand," Arabella said, overwhelmed with a familiar sense of fondness as she gazed at the golden-haired man across from her. She liked the laugh-lines that had scored themselves around his blue eyes: they hadn't been there when she first saw him, and his curls had been more carefully trimmed then, too. But one thing had remained constant about him since she knew him—the kindness that lurked at the back of his eyes.

"I'm quite certain I don't understand," said Mikkel. "It's why I asked. What on earth did they offer you as bait to become a Time Corp ensign alongside me and put your life in danger every day?"

"I wasn't offered bait to accompany you, my darling," said Arabella. "Accompanying you *was* the bait."

Mikkel looked as though he was caught between rue and laughter. "Your employers used me as bait to corrupt you?"

Arabella, who had operated both outside of and alongside the Universal Law for most of her life, fixed him with her primmest look. "I like to think that I was already pretty fairly headed along the path I was going to take before my employers offered me a way to do what I wanted to do anyway."

"What was it that you wanted to do?"

"Meet you, of course," said Arabella, delighting in both the breath she saw suddenly catch, and the faint ruddiness to Mikkel's cheeks. "I'd been waiting for years. Of course, when I finally did meet you in person properly, it was rather overwhelming—"

"You sent me flying," interrupted Mikkel, making a valiant comeback.

"Well, I wasn't prepared to see quite so much of you," Arabella protested. "And I was used to having a screen between us, so your physical presence was rather...awe-inspiring."

"I wouldn't have guessed it from your bearing."

"I'm very glad to hear it," Arabella said. "I was trying desperately to be business-like. At that point I didn't know I really would marry you; I just wanted to be the one to work with you. Are you sure you don't want to see the noticeboard, my darling?"

"I'm not even faintly interested in the noticeboard," Mikkel remarked. "I very much want to know more about how your employers used me as bait to employ you."

"As I said before, it's rather a long story."

Mikkel turned a particularly melting look on her. "I assume it starts at the point where you fell in love with me."

"No, it starts with gardening," Arabella said firmly. "Are you sure you wouldn't like to check the noticeboard first?"

"I've become used to the feeling of being herded," Mikkel told her. "But you shouldn't imagine that means I like it. What exactly is it you want me to see on the noticeboard?"

"I thought you might be interested to see that a new Fixed Point formed overnight, my darling. It's pertinent to what you're asking about."

Mikkel narrowed his eyes at her, but she saw the curve of his lower lip as he tried to stifle the smile. "Something that just happened is pertinent to both gardening and how you ended up on my ship?" he asked, briefly scanning the noticeboard. His brows went up. "Good heavens."

"Yes," said Arabella cheerfully. "Isn't it interesting?"

"I'm still more interested in how I was used as bait to induce you to put yourself at the beck and call of shadowy employers who not only permit you to break universal laws but positively *encourage* it."

"Ah," said Arabella. "Well, to understand that, you need to understand—"

"Gardening. Yes, so you said."

"No, my darling; first you need to understand that I like to know the rules, but I don't always follow them. I just like to know what the consequences are for not following them so I can make my own decisions. Why are you kissing me?"

"Because you're my favourite anarchist. What is the second thing I need to understand?"

"The second thing you need to understand is exactly how the art of pyromaniac gardening works..."

MEMENTO MORI: REDUX

THERE WAS A CERTAIN CALMNESS TO SIX O'CLOCK IN THE morning, no matter whether the time occurred world-side, where a sun or suns could be guaranteed to be rising or about to be rising, or onboard any ship or orbiting apparatus that went by its own relative time.

Peaceful, quiet, and entirely unhurried moments ticked heavily by, one by one, as soft shadows crept across the wall opposite the window simulator Selroy had installed in his entirely underground room. He had installed it in order to trick his Eighth World brain that he had some species of access to the outside world on those days he didn't leave his quarters, and beside the smug pleasure it gave him to so easily hack his own bodily chemistry, it provided for a pleasant past-time in the morning as he limbered up his brain to begin work for the day.

By the time the bars of shadow and light had progressed to the corner of his sleeping closet, Selroy's brain, bright and warm and quick-moving, would be ready to begin work for the day. At 06:15 by Local Relative Time here in the Incursion Specialist's underground, Selroy would rise from his prone position like a vampire in its coffin, the corded green stalks of his hair pointing straight at the ceiling and his angular shoulders slightly hunched in the same direction.

This morning was no different: 06:15 LRT arrived in a steady, soft progression of fake dawn-light across the wall, and Selroy sat straight up in his bed, green, stalky hair pointing straight at the ceiling.

This morning, however, there was one slight difference. When Selroy padded out into his workshop, blinking mildly to clear the sleep from his eye implants, the corner of the room was missing. Selroy stared at that missing piece for the space of a few moments, his mind running through various scenarios, then went on through to his kitchen.

The matter was urgent, but unless he fed himself, he wouldn't be in optimal shape to do what needed to be done. Missing reality was a very bad sign, even if there wasn't a lot of it missing:

the fact that it was missing was enough to signal one of only two different problems.

Best case scenario, someone, somewhere out in the universe, had caused a hiccough in the fabric of time and space that would cause Time Corp and the Incursion Specialists alike a headache, and keep Selroy up for a week in fixing it.

Worst case scenario...

Selroy trod softly back into his workroom with a nutrient-rich drink in one hand and a biscuit in the other, and opened his console. It lit up at once, replete with the usual displays and lights in a pleasing combination of teal and lemon, but around the edges warning lights in purple immediately glowed.

He touched the screen with a curious feeling of finality, and saw his worst case scenario in every interconnected warning light that formed an equation with a single, inevitable conclusion.

Selroy laid a finger over his comm and said, "Director Bell. I need to talk to you."

Someone toggled the comms on and off, then on again in an unwary—perhaps a somnolent—movement, and a mumble of noise in the background said something like, "Who is it?"

Director Bell's voice muttered, "The one with the green hair, dear. Go back to sleep."

Selroy waited patiently. If he'd had friends, they would probably have called him Celery. Since he didn't, he went by an assortment of appellations that ranged anywhere from *sir* to *the weird one with green hair*. Selroy didn't mind the different names, so long as they were intuitive enough to be easily grasped: he couldn't change his hair colour, and in general he was the most senior person in any given room, though he had no official rank. People often tended to say things he didn't understand, and it was a relief at least not to have to guess if they were speaking to him or not.

Finally, Director Bell's voice said, heavy with sleep, "Selroy? Is that you?"

"Yes."

There was a brief pause, and Director Bell said impatiently, "Well?"

"Yes, it's me. Selroy." Selroy cleared his throat.

"What is the *problem*, Selroy?"

"Oh," said Selroy. He cleared his throat and said again, "Yes. Well. It seems that the universe is ending today."

"I beg your pardon?" said Director Bell, coldly.

"The universe is ending: I've been tracking changes in the timestream and the Other Zone for half an hour now, and I'm quite certain."

"Are you joking—no, of course you're not joking; you wouldn't know how. You're—you're *absolutely certain?*"

"Yes, sir."

"How long have we got?" asked Bell. From the change in his speech patterns, Selroy guessed that the man had risen and was now dressing hurriedly.

"I should think we've got about fifteen hours before things start falling to pieces in a meaningful sort of way," Selroy said, his mind ranging over the different strands of information available on his dashboard. "There should be signs of decay already: you'll notice it around the Facility sooner or later."

Bell's voice came sharp and hard. "What do you mean by falling to pieces? Is the timestream already at risk? Our mechanisms?"

"The timestream," agreed Selroy. "And everything else. Things are starting to cease to exist."

There was another pause; this one longer. Undoubtedly Director Bell was looking at his own console, in which case he could see a report of what Selroy had already seen in his own workshop.

This time, Director Bell sounded as if he was finding it hard to breathe when he spoke. "And this has something to do with the bits of the Facility that are apparently missing?"

"No; the bits of the Facility that are missing have to do with the universe ending today. They're a product, not causative."

"The universe—" Director Bell stopped, as though frustrated, and began again. "How can the universe be ending?"

"It was bound to happen someday," opined Selroy. "It shouldn't have been today, but here we are."

"Selroy," said Director Bell, and by the weary sound of his voice, Selroy guessed that he had finally found the right question to ask instead of the inane ones he had hitherto been asking, "*why* is the universe ending today?"

Tuan Li woke with a gentle feeling of wellbeing that lasted for roughly three seconds after he opened his eyes and smiled at the curved, closer-than-usual ceiling above him. He wasn't aboard the *TCS Slider*; he was aboard the *Upsydaisy*—finally, and properly.

For those three seconds, he was as contentedly warm on the outside as he was on the inside; then a small, angular whirlwind with too many sharp edges and far too little care exploded into the room and launched itself onto him.

Tuan gasped as Kez's full weight drove itself into his stomach, creating the agony of a thorough winding while depriving him of the breath to fully express that agony. Her weight wasn't a sizeable number, despite her currently nineteen years, but as with every other aspect of Kez, size was very much deceptive, and served merely as a funnel-like conduit by which to channel all of her energy into a single, potent force.

"'Allo, TuanTuan," she said, grinning down at him. "Ain't you glad you're 'ere?"

Tuan groaned on an indrawn breath, and Kez wriggled until she was sitting next to him instead of on top of him. He hoped for a reprieve, but the movement was only so that she could flop down and hug him tightly enough to force the groan back out of him again.

"Missed you, TuanTuan," she said.

TuanTuan said "ouch" as she bit his arm, but couldn't help

the glad smile spreading over his face again. "Is that what it means?" he asked. "Biting me?"

"Means I'm glad to see you," she said, in a muffled voice.

"There are other ways to tell people you miss them," Tuan said, but he wrapped his arms around her and returned the hug with all the gladness in his heart, squeezing his eyes shut to prevent her seeing the tears that had gathered there. She probably already knew, but Tuan would prefer not to actually weep on her.

"Yeah?" Kez pulled away a little just as he opened his eyes, but only to rest her folded arms on his chest and her chin on her arms. She grinned at him. "Missed me, didn't ya?"

"I always miss you," Tuan said.

Again, Kez moved; this time she wriggled forward a little and planted a very small, very precise kiss on his nose. Tuan froze; blinked. Kez sat up and he followed her, and this time he was looking down at her, as incapable of words as before.

Without knowing exactly what he was saying, he finally said again, "I always—I always miss you."

"You never say it, though," Kez said. "That's the first time. Fort I was the only one."

"Where did you learn...that?" Tuan asked, touching his nose.

"Seen Arabella wiv Mikkel," explained Kez. "I'm not a kid, you know."

"You can't tell me Arabella and Mikkel go around kissing like that," Tuan said. He had been assigned to the *TCS Slider* for service—Mikkel's ship—which meant that he had also seen Arabella and Mikkel together when they thought they weren't observed.

"Yeah, but it's wot she does when he does summink she likes," Kez said. "Collars 'im and pops one on 'is snoot."

"You don't—you don't go around doing that to everyone who does something you like, do you?" asked Tuan, rather worried.

Kez stared at him. "'Course not," she said. "Ain't anyone else but you who does stuff I like."

"But what if there was?" pressed Tuan. He was unsure of how to get the answer he wanted other than by outright demanding that Kez not kiss anyone but himself, and he was rather afraid she might hit him if he said that. "Would you kiss them, too?"

Unexpectedly, Kez laughed. "Ain't met anyone as clever as you, TuanTuan," she said. "But you're also flamin' stupid sometimes. 'F anyone else did what you do, I wouldn't like it, 'cos it wouldn't be you."

There it was, realised Selroy. The actual question Bell had wanted to ask from the start. He wished, not for the first time, that people would ask what they wanted to know in the first place instead of asking questions all around it, as if they expected him to guess what they were asking.

"Someone untethered two Fixed Points at once," he said. "I don't know which two, because they no longer exist. The universe has split into three versions of itself, and whichever one we're in is falling apart. The other ones probably are, too, just not as quickly as this one. It's one thing to unfix one Point; unfixing two at once is just asking for trouble."

There was silence on the other end of the comm for a moment or two, then someone bustled through the door. Director Bell, Selroy saw, as he turned to greet the interloper. He didn't know why the man had to come to Selroy's workspace: there was nothing they could discuss face to face that they couldn't have talked about over the comms.

Behind Bell was a v-formation of Very Important Men who were tousle-headed, half-dressed, and highly alarmed.

"You'd better have a good explanation for this," Bell said. "Because—"

"I already told you," said Selroy, rather annoyed. "The universe is falling apart. If you don't want to know about it, you shouldn't have asked. It doesn't need your permission."

A babble of sound rose into the air, to be split by one central voice that bellowed, "*Cut it out!*"

An uneasy silence fell; grew in both unease and awkwardness. Selroy, who didn't really care about awkwardness or unease, said into the silence, "It won't do any good standing around here. I mean, it won't do any good standing around anywhere else, either, but I'm going to be rather busy and you're all in the way."

"Selroy," said one of the men, "what do you mean, it won't do any good? What can we do to stop this?"

"You can't," Selroy said simply. "It'll happen no matter what we do. Unless we get knitted back into the other timelines, that is; and in that case, none of us will exist in the state we currently do anyway."

"How do we knit ourselves back into the original timeline, then?" asked Bell.

"We don't," said Selroy. "Well, we can't: no time."

Bell sounded rather strangled. "How do we stop ourselves dying?"

"Can't do that, either," Selroy said.

"Selroy," Bell said, through his teeth, "*What are you going to do?*"

"I thought I might work on the Newlands Box," Selroy said. "I would have liked to have had more time on it, but I can probably do a decent job on it anyway, with the time I have left."

"The Newlands Box is a glorified message box that hasn't got anything to do with time, space, or the death of the known universe," Bell grated. "I refuse to allow you to work on it!"

"I hope you won't," said Selroy, running through the three viable scenarios wherein he could once more get his lab to himself and secure all the resources he needed. "It would really make things difficult for me and wouldn't help you at all."

One of the scenarios Selroy had in mind involved Bell's death, and he would much rather not kill the man. Death was messy and itchy and made it hard to concentrate; Selroy wanted to concentrate as best as he could. If Bell and the others would only leave him alone, it would be much easier to begin. He had reported the situation to them, and now it would be preferable if they would leave him alone to work. There was so little time left.

"I need to concentrate now," he told Bell. Sometimes being straightforward seemed to work particularly well, and sometimes it didn't: Selroy simply had no more time to waste. "If you're going to ask more questions, please make sure you ask important ones."

"What is being done about *reality as a whole*?"

That at least was an important question. Selroy unlocked the Newlands Box and connected it to his console, and as he did, said over his shoulder, "Remember those aberrations you've been keeping an eye on?"

"I'm aware of them," said Bell, and Selroy was pretty sure he was still speaking between his teeth. "So is the Time Corp, if that matters."

"Time Corp always matters," said Selroy. "But they're stuck to their Core, and it isn't always accurate—especially now. That's why I came to work for the Incursion Specialists instead: I wanted to meet those two aberrations. They're the only ones who can stop this from happening in the original timeline, too. I'm going to send them help."

"Send...*them* help? Why? And *how*?"

Selroy kindly ignored the first two questions. Bell always did need help asking the right questions. "There's the Newlands Box," he said. "I'll get that finished and try to find a way to ship it off. It won't stop the universe from ending here in this reality, but it might stop it in the original."

"Selroy," said another of the men, breathing too heavily, "we want to know what you're going to do to fix *this reality*?"

"Nothing," Selroy repeated. "We're not even original. So long as the original universe stays around, we'll all be there in one form or another."

"You want us to sit around and wait for the universe to fall apart?"

"You can do what you like," Selroy said, by way of offering a sop. "Have a cup of tea; eat a biscuit. It won't matter. You might as well do something enjoyable. I don't need your help."

"Thank you," said Bell grimly, "but I'll stay, all the same."

Tuan didn't mean to, but he found himself tugging at the hair behind his ear, his face warm.

Kez gave her deep little crow of laughter and said, "Told you. I ain't a kid anymore."

Tuan would have liked to try and kiss her properly, but a shadow fell by the hatch and Marx's dry voice said, "There's breakfast in the mess-room; we'll discuss sorting out some real quarters for you once you're finished eating."

He didn't wait to hear them reply; didn't stop to ask why the two of them were sitting nose-to-nose, either, but Tuan didn't dare to stay where he was. Maybe one day he'd be as brave as Kez when it came to Marx, but he thought he'd have to trust Marx significantly more in order to be able to do so, and he was rather sure that Kez was the only one who had reason to trust Marx to that necessary extent.

Tuan cleared his throat and wriggled off the bed. He pulled on a jumper he knew to be Kez's favourite, and asked through the cable-knit fuzz of it, "Why did you two just steal the Newlands Box again?"

"Saw a kerfuffle in the Core an' knew we were s'posed to do it."

"That's—that's no reason to go doing things," Tuan said, emerging from the jumper with the hair on his neck standing on end. "Time Corp is sure to catch you if you go around doing things like that! They have access to the Core too, you know."

"'Course!" scoffed Kez. "But they don't know we got access to it, see? Works out well. We just try to do stuff in an unexpected way."

"How can you do things in enough of an unexpected way to

confuse Time Corp if they already know you're going to be there?"

"That's the thing," said Kez, chuckling again. "Don't reckon you understand wot 'appens, TuanTuan. The Core just records stuff an' updates as it 'appens: they can't update stuff quickly enough if we're always changin' our minds. An' sometimes while it thinks we're doin' summink, we're doin' summink else."

"I vaguely follow that," said Tuan. "But that still doesn't explain how you knew you were going to do something because you saw it in the Core, did it, and still weren't caught in time."

"Cos the Core doesn't know it's us, of course," Kez told him. "We know it's us wot's doin' it, but they don't. They just record it as summink that happened."

"What about the times when they know it's you? There are loads of direct references to you in the Core!"

"Yeah, but 'ow many of them is Fixed Points?" countered Kez, grinning. "Anyway, look at it like this, TuanTuan: today we pinched the Newlands Box, but we also pinched you, too."

"You didn't steal me, I came along!" Tuan said indignantly. He had fought very hard to be allowed to come along, too; it had taken years for Marx to agree to it, and while Tuan thought he might, distantly, understand the reasons as to why, he still resented that achievement being taken away from him.

"Yeah, but the Core don't know that," pointed out Kez. "It thinks someone made away wiv you, see? So instead av goin' there wiv the idea of stealin' you, we'd go there wiv the idea of stealin' the box!"

Tuan stared at her for a very long time before he asked, "Is that what you did?"

"Nah," said Kez, grinning. "We just wanted the box. We've been chasin' it around for a while. Oi. You get breakfast; I gotta check on summink."

. . .

Selroy didn't so much find himself left alone as he studiously and determinedly ignored everyone in the room until they stopped asking questions of him and left him alone to do what he had to do. One or two nagging annoyances remained in the room, but Selroy was very good at ignoring persistent niggles, and he continued to do so, grateful for his comfortable quarters at the WAOF's Incursion Specialist Facility that meant it was extremely unlikely that any of those niggling annoyances would ever be waving a weapon in his direction.

What did he need to do? First, thought Selroy, he needed to make sure he knew where those two aberrations were. He also needed to pinpoint where the trouble had begun, but that wasn't possible; the Fixed Points that existed in another reality—the unfixing of which had created his own reality—didn't exist here. In order to save the real universe, he would need to make use of the only people besides himself who seemed to be able to make changes and cause waves in other realities. He had already been tracking the two aberrations for some time, insofar as they *could* be tracked, which wasn't much, and he wasn't quite certain of his ability to find them today.

He searched his system for them, momentarily encountering a hiccough that suggested there might, in another reality, be *three* aberrations, then found exactly what he was looking for. There they were, about to do something that would make the timeline bulge a bit. Selroy hoped that meant they were already working on the same thing he was working on. It would be nice not to have to explain too much: he'd already been pretty specific with the files he put in the Newlands Box, after all.

"What *are* you doing?" demanded Bell, looking over his shoulder.

Selroy hunched that shoulder, but since it sometimes helped to talk things through aloud, he said, "These two. They've been causing incursions since I've had access to this data: they've made reality a bit thin in a few places, too. If anyone can make a hole in reality big enough to push a box through, it's these two."

"A hole...in *reality*? Selroy, you just told me that the universe is falling apart and you want to let two aberrations make a *hole in reality*?"

"If my calculations are correct, there's a point at which they've stolen the Newlands Box—or their version of it—three times. If they try to push it through there, I've got a very good hunch that it'll make it through the original timestream without causing too much damage."

"*A hunch*?"

"A very good one," pointed out Selroy.

"Without *too much damage*?" choked Bell.

"If you're experiencing disorientation, it's perfectly normal," Selroy said. "You could be approaching disintegration before the surrounding environment. A little unusual, but—"

"I am not experiencing disorientation!" snapped Bell. "I am experiencing disbelief that you seem to think a *hunch* and *not too much damage* are enough to go by!"

"My hunches are measured at an accuracy of ninety-nine point eight percent," said Selroy. "In fact, they're not really hunches, but people don't usually understand when I tell them how my mind works, so—"

"Why," said Bell, in a deceptively gentle voice, "are you wasting time trying to push a *box* through to the original timeline?"

"I'm not," Selroy said. "I'm going to push it through to those two in our reality with a few instructions to help them out. It looks like they're already experiencing an incursion of their own, so they'll most likely know what to do with the box if I give them a few pointers. They'll push it through to the original timestream in one of the thinner areas."

Bell pinched the bridge of his nose. "Selroy, why are *they* bothering to try and push a box through to the original timestream?"

"I would assume that they left themselves a message that they had to do it," said Selroy. "That's what the data would indicate. Or at least, something that made them cognisant of the other realities, and the disintegration of the Fixed Points. If I was them, I would have tried to get to this reality to see where it differed from mine, and then fix it from their own."

He could link the Newlands Box with other realities; fill it with information that didn't exist in the original reality, but he couldn't send it into another reality. But Selroy was quite certain that his two aberrations could send it into the original reality: everything was connected to them, after all. He was also quite certain that they were the only ones who could do anything with a box pre-programmed with everything needed to save time, reality, and the original universe.

Well, *almost* everything.

Tuan had just settled himself in the co-pilot's chair at the *Upsy-daisy*'s console when Kez kicked open the hatch door and pushed him out of that position of comfort. She sat down in it herself and spun to face Marx.

Tuan said, "Ow," peaceably and sat down on the floor at her feet instead, which particular instance of devotion Kez rewarded by tugging on his hair with both hands, the Newlands Box sitting lopsidedly in her lap.

"Oi," she said to Marx. "There's summink in the Box."

"What about it?" asked Marx, flipping switches on the *Upsy-daisy*'s console.

He wasn't really paying attention, Tuan thought, which was rather dangerous. Kez tended to do unexpected things when people didn't pay attention to her, no matter how old she was.

Still without looking up, Marx said, "We already know it's a recording device. It's got all of Uncle Li's contacts on it."

"And his blackmail source files," added Tuan, tilting his head back to look at Kez. "I stopped looking at those yesterday, though. It has a good bit of useful tech on there, too."

"Not anymore, it don't," said Kez grimly, leaning her arms on

Tuan's head instead of pulling his hair. "All them files an' records and speakin' bits an' stuff? They're gone. Someone else is speakin' instead. Ain't no pictures, either."

Marx abandoned his console, and swung his chair to face them. "All right, I'll bite. Who is it?"

"You'll see," said Kez, and started the Box.

A voice crackled out of the box, and the hair on Tuan's neck stood up for the second or third time that day, because it was Kez's voice.

"This thing on? 'Ow's it work? Oh, right; I just talk. 'Allo."

"Get on with it, kid," said Marx's voice, from the box.

He and Kez exchanged a glance, then they both turned suspicious, accusatory looks on Tuan. Luckily for Tuan, he knew that the suspicion wasn't directed at him—only the accusation. They wanted to know what was happening, and how, and that was his job.

"I don't—I don't know," he said helplessly.

"We've only got ten minutes," continued Marx's voice.

"Oh yeah," said the Kez-in-the-box. "Hey Marx, it's me, Kez."

"It's me, kid."

So whatever time or place this bit of speaking was from, they knew they were talking to themselves, and had meant for the box to be exactly where it was, at exactly the time it was there.

That, supposed Tuan, was something.

Kez-in-the-box said, "It's both of us, anyway, talkin' to— talkin' to—well, both of us, I s'pose. An' TuanTuan."

"His name is Tuan. He's not your pet."

The Kez who was in the cabin with them grinned, but that grin faded quickly when Kez-in-the-box said, with a faint tremor in her voice, "Oi, TuanTuan. You don't exist 'ere. Ain't real nice. You should've tried 'arder."

"He does exist," said Marx-in-the-Box, as Marx began to look more grim than he had before. Tuan, who had frozen a little, felt oddly comforted by that grimness. "He just made different choices. Look, shut up, kid; I'll do the talking. The thing is that there's a Fixed Point—well, it was a Fixed Point, but someone has been playing around with it and things have gotten a bit confusing. There's a whole alternate timeline in place and I don't know if we'll be able to push the Box through even if we manage to find a point that's weak enough to try."

"But we reckon if we find the right place—y'know, where we've stole the Box enough times—it'll be enough to get the message through," cut in Kez-in-the-Box. "Summink about time an' space bein' thinner there."

"The Box won't do you much good, but if you can get it back to yourselves before the Fixed Points start getting unfixed—"

Tuan's stomach sank. Fixed Points. And not just Fixed Points, but Fixed Points that were becoming unfixed...

"Then we got a chance to fix it all," said Kez-in-the-Box, her voice sharp and urgent.

"The important thing is that you need to make sure that the Fixed Points stay fixed."

"All of 'em," Kez-in-the-Box said, her voice more than usually threatening.

"Yes, all of 'em. Better listen carefully, because once the Fixed Points are unfixed, your Core isn't going to tell you the things you need to know to make them fixed again."

"Already seen that," muttered Kez, scowling at the Box.

Kez-in-the-Box, interrupting, said, "An' if you don't, we're gunna die. We're gunna be in the wrong timeline and we're gunna die."

Tuan sat up very straight. There it was: the Thing he needed to know to start making sense of all of this. Fixed Points had been unfixed, and Kez said that this iteration of them was in the wrong timeline, not that they were somewhere else in time, which meant that—

"Oh no," said Tuan. "You split reality. You're not supposed to split reality!"

Beneath his voice, the box continued to speak with Marx's

voice. "You'll need everyone: Arabella, Mikkel, Tuan—heck, bring in Vladivostok, too. That Sergeant might help, too; you never know. We can't go back to the Fixed Points without unfixing 'em just by being there. That's why things went so badly in this timeline."

"An' we're gunna die," said Kez-in-the-Box, her voice gruff.

"Possibly. Probably. Yeah, we're gunna die."

"Don't even know wot mucker done it."

"Not for sure, anyway. We've narrowed it down to the Holstrom Institute, a special branch of the WAOF—Incursion Specialists, they call themselves; you'll meet 'em later—or Uncle Cheng."

"But first you gotta find the Fixed Points—" interrupted Kez-in-the-Box.

"—before whoever it is finds them and starts undoing them."

"—an' when you find 'em, you have to make sure everything 'appens like it's meant to 'appen. Only you can't go there yourselves—"

Tuan nodded vehemently, a cold shudder creeping up his back.

"—because that will be enough to unfix 'em. Trust us. And if you can find out who's doing it and stop them—that'll make life easier for you."

Sharply, Kez-in-the-Box said, "Oi. Should that be doin' that?"

"Nope. Don't touch it."

"Ain't gunna touch it! Anyway, we—oo-er! Marx!"

A cold hand gripped Tuan's simu-wool-clad shoulder, and he reached back to pull both of Kez's arms around his neck, drawing her closer.

With a dreadfully grim finality, Marx-in-the-Box said, "That's torn it. C'mmere, kid."

"Oo-er! Marx, lookit—! Marx!"

Kez breathed just a bit too quickly in his ear, and Tuan found that he was gripping her arms as if he could save that other version of Kez from whatever was dogging her.

But he couldn't reach out to that other Kez, and Marx-in-the-Box said roughly, "It's okay, kid. I got you. Close your eyes. It's oka—"

"What?" demanded Bell, his voice alarmed.

Selroy, who had sighed, said with a little melancholy, "I can't give the aberrations the point of diversion for this reality. I told you that."

He would have liked to have provided everything: *Selroy, Saviour of the Universe* sounded quite nice. But he had access only to his own reality, and at best a vague idea of what could be happening in other realities. Incursions were only, after all, indicators, and couldn't be said to give a complete picture of what may or may not be happening in another reality.

Still, the point of divergence for this reality, if knit back together with the original timeline, would certainly resolve the issues of *one* Fixed Point, and hopefully stabilise the original timeline for long enough to resolve the others. The aberrations themselves could hopefully be trusted to find the point of difference; Selroy was merely providing the method of transmission for that information.

His console, which had been processing vast amounts of data in order to find the coming incursion, chirped at him with a result and a warning. He ignored the warning and went on to the result: a two-line blurb of information that listed time, co-ordinates, and size of incursion.

"Ah!" he said in satisfaction.

A few of his instruments began to pulse purple on the console, warning that reality in the room had lost coherency a little more quickly than the previous speed of disintegration would have suggested, and a sudden wild babble of chatter behind him suggested that it had done so noticeably.

Selroy ignored the chatter and happily plugged the box into his console properly.

A shadow, looming at his shoulder, demanded, "What's that? What are you doing with that?"

"Don't stand there," said Selroy to the orange-haired man suddenly by his side. "There are bits missing. I've upset the balance in the room a bit: I had to get a piece of information that makes things a bit more wobbly when someone knows it."

The man screamed and did a frantic dance sideways, a blue arc of disintegrating trouser leg floating in the air for a moment before it disappeared. The wall beside which he had been standing now showed a gaping hole right through to the inside of the wall. Before much longer, it would probably show the next room. Selroy wondered if he would still be whole himself when it came to the stage of being able to see into the foundations.

The man with orange hair finally achieved balance again and said sharply, "Did you do that?"

"Of course not," Selroy said. "The universe is disintegrating; it was always going to disintegrate there first. It just happened a bit more quickly because of me."

"Then stop doing that!"

"That's not logical," said Selroy, going back to the Box. "Whether or not I stop, the disintegration will continue. If you don't like it, move."

"*Stop*," said the man with orange hair, through his teeth.

Bell shifted in his seat, irritating Selroy, then froze. "I suggest you put that away," he said. "Selroy, *move!*"

Selroy saw no reason why he should move, but it seemed as though his body had other thoughts. First it jerked forward, prompting a searing pain that was exactly in synch with the sudden, violent melting of the console in front of him, then it flopped back as though his spine had turned to warm treacle.

He stared at the splattering of purple mixing with melted console, then down at the rather devastating hole in the shoulder of his shirt that still smoked and smelt vaguely like barbeque.

And Selroy realised, far too late, that one of his niggling annoyances was now, in fact, waving a weapon.

There was only silence: silence that stretched out for a very long time until Kez said in Tuan's ear, "We're gunna die."

Tuan would have tried to reassure her properly if he'd heard the rough scratchiness in her voice that meant she was really concerned. Since he hadn't, he only gazed back up at her and said, "No. I won't let you."

She stared at him, then grinned, and loosened her grip around his neck. She was scared, but not terrified. That was good.

"Still—" Even Marx looked thoughtful. "Think it's a trick?"

"No," said Tuan. He reached over his shoulder to tap the lid of the Box with one finger. "Even the outside of the Box—it's not the same as it was."

"What do you mean, it's not the same?"

"The pattern is different." Tuan tilted it for Marx to see. He'd seen the Newlands Box once or twice before; its lid had always been picked out in green from a brown and gold background. Now, however, that random pattern had been replaced with ancient Seventh World characters.

"Wot's it say?" demanded Kez.

Since Tuan knew how well she spoke Seventh World dialect, he only blinked at her.

"I can *speak* it," Kez protested. "Never said I could *read* it!"

"It's a proverb," Tuan said. In light of what they had just heard from the Newlands Box, it was a rather ominous inscription. "It's the Seventh World equivalent of that ancient Latin phrase—"

"*Memento mori*," Marx said grimly.

"You didn't know about the recording when you stole it, did you?" Tuan said.

"Nope," said Kez. "It wasn't there last time we stole it, and I reckon it might not be there next time we steal it, either. It's a new thing, like when the Core updates itself through all of time and reality."

"The Core is meant to be the only thing in the universe that can do that," Tuan said, and his voice sounded slightly accusatory to his own ears.

"Maybe it's summink you made in another reality and sent to us," said Kez in a soothing voice that suggested she knew exactly why he felt annoyed at the idea.

"If I'd known you wanted something like that, I would have worked on making it, but—"

"Reckon we're really gunna die?"

"No," said Marx, and his eyes met Tuan's. "Why else would we have the Box? We sent it to ourselves so that we can do something about dying. What I want to know is what we're talking about when we say *another timeline*."

"That..." began Tuan, tugging at the hair behind his ear. "That is pretty bad news. If Fixed Points are being altered, new realities will be splitting from the original: *another timeline* could be one of those versions of reality that we accessed to try and realign the Fixed Points."

"'Oo said it was our job?" Kez muttered. "Go jumpin' around in time and space and suddenly everyone wants you to fix problems when they ain't tryin' to kill you."

"I doubt anyone else knows," Tuan told her. "If I'm right, the only reason we know about it is that one of *our* Fixed Points has been altered."

"Rude, that," said Marx, his mouth grim.

"*Flamin'* rude," agreed Kez. "Wot you gunna do about it, TuanTuan?"

Tuan choked a little as he said, "I'm sorry, what?"

"You're the science man," said Marx. "That's why we brought you along. That can be your job; sounds like we're going to be a bit busy trying not to die in another timeline."

"Wot I wanna know," said Kez, frowning, "is if we know

we're gunna die if we go into another sorta branchy reality, how come we go over to that reality? We know we gotta fix up some Fixed Points before some mucker messes wiv 'em—so why don't we go do that, eh? Stay in our own reality an' fix it from 'ere?"

"Because we don't know which ones are unfixed," said Tuan. There was a distinctly sinking feeling in his stomach. He thought he understood, dimly, why they had just gotten a message from Kez and Marx in another timeline. "I think—I'm pretty sure we won't be able to see the divergence on our side. It'll probably be pretty noticeable to us from the other side once we get there, though. The other reality, I mean."

"Reckon I better check up on the Other Zone before we go messin' about wiv this too much," opined Kez. "Could be a trap or summink. Giv'us a tick; I'll go 'ave a look."

Tuan met Marx's eyes, feeling a faint touch of relief. A trap would be so much easier to deal with than actual Fixed Points— but Tuan didn't see how it was possible for someone to have gotten hold of Marx and Kez's voices and vocal reflexes so accurately as to make a recording so utterly believable.

"Take it easy out there, kid," said Marx. "We'll be waiting here. Don't be gone long."

"Yeah, yeah," Kez said. "Ain't me first time, you know."

Tuan had seen her disappear and appear with barely a missing patch of time to show that she'd been gone for hours—or days, or weeks—and he was quite familiar with what to expect. He didn't expect Kez to flicker for a bare instant, then scream, short and ragged, and whirl herself around and behind Marx, her arms wrapped around her head.

Marx and Tuan stared at each other for a stunned moment that was filled with the quick, panting breath of Kez as she cradled her head in her arms, then Tuan crouched beside her, alarmed. He hadn't seen her like this for years: small and terrified and entirely feral.

"Kez. *Kez.* What's wrong? What's happening?"

Kez lifted her head, but she didn't look properly at him: her eyes looked right through him and at something only she could see. Marx didn't make a move to crouch down and comfort her, and it took Tuan only a moment to see why: she was using his legs as a back-guard, pushed right up against them like she might against a wall, and the knuckles of Marx's fingers just brushed the top of her head.

"Talk, kid," Marx said, looking down at her.

"Ain't nothin' there," Kez said, her fingers clinging to Tuan's arm through the simu-wool of his jumper. "The Other Zone's there all right, but the timestream's just...disappearin'. Little bits floatin' off into nothin'. Even this bit wiv us, right now: if we don't move soon, we're gunna unravel."

Tuan took in a trembling breath, and hoped that his hand didn't tremble when he gripped it around hers. "They—you—the box said *two* Fixed Points. One at a time would cause problems, but two at once could potentially—potentially—"

"Split the universe?" finished Marx.

"They all split the universe," said Tuan, his brain buzzing. "Potentially, I mean. Theoretically. Fixed Points are fixed because they need to happen for the universe to continue as we know it. Any smaller changes still flow back into the same old timestream and keep it flowing the way they were meant to. But undoing a Fixed Point is like—it's like blowing up part of the stream and redirecting it into another stream-bed."

"We've got time running in a different direction?"

"Yes, but we've still got it running in the same direction, as well," Tuan told him, looking up into Marx's grim eyes. "That's why we're still here as well. We've got two different directions; the stream is split."

"So if someone broke two Fixed Points at once—"

"Yes," said Tuan. "It'd be like trying to blow up another part of the stream. The whole lot would just make a big mess."

"It ain't a big mess," Kez said, some semblance of reason returning to her mirror-like eyes. "It's just *fallin' apart*. An' there's stuff tricklin' all back through the timestream, too. Whatever was 'appenin' when that recording was put in the Newlands Box, I reckon—"

"It's happening now," Marx said grimly. "Or spreading back to now, at any rate. That explains the mess we've been seeing in the Core lately. I thought we'd have a bit more time to work it out before anything really bad happened. Kid—*kid*. Which direction was the disintegration?"

Kez stared at him for a moment, then said, "No direction. Little bits just gone everywhere—can't even tell when it's gunna 'appen; stuff just vanishes."

Tuan felt the warmth of something in his left hand, growing hotter and hotter, and looked down blankly at the Newlands Box. It still bore the inscription in Seventh World script; an inscription that roughly equated to *memento mori*, but now there was a tangible energy to it that made him open it quickly.

"Oh," he said, staring down at myriad files that had not been there a moment ago. "I think we ought to have another look at this, first."

"Selroy," said Bell grimly. "Are you all right?"

"I should think I'll be all right for another ten minutes if my cells don't begin to reform," said Selroy, and took a few moments to appreciate the woolly feeling of his tongue in his mouth. He didn't remember it feeling like that before. "If they do, I'll likely be all right for a good hour or so without medical assistance."

"You're not going to get any assistance," said the orange-haired man. "You're going to sit there and figure out how to save us all."

Selroy opened his mouth, caught Bell's granite-hard eyes, and went back to contemplating his tongue.

"You're not thinking straight, Jonas," said Bell. His voice was commanding and certain; he probably used the same voice with small children and animals, as well as the men under his command.

It probably also worked more often than not.

This time, it did not.

"Shut up, Bell," the orange-haired man said.

"If you concentrate on your breathing for a while, you'll be able to think more logically," suggested Selroy, since the commanding voice hadn't worked. In his experience, it was difficult to address a problem when one's body and brain were at odds with what was going on.

"If you concentrate on your work for a while, you'll be able to go on breathing," Jonas suggested in return.

The man was still breathing too quickly, Selroy noticed, and his face was a mottled shade of red that was very much at odds with his hair.

"No matter how much I concentrate on my work, the same thing will happen in the end," he told Jonas. "Waving a weapon around isn't going to change that. Nothing is going to change it."

"It'll change how long you live," Jonas snarled, starting across the room with all the subtlety of a bull charging. "So if it's all right with you, we're going to get to work on saving the universe."

"Oh, that's all right," said Selroy, rather hazily. He could feel the prickliness of his skin cells forming barriers around the outsides of the wound, but it would take a little while before his full function of thought returned to him. "I'll just be off, then."

"Selroy," Bell said, in a hiss, "stay where you are and *don't move!*"

That, considered Selroy, made absolutely no sense at all. His work on the Newlands Box was by no means complete, and he had very little time in which to finish it.

So Selroy reached out a shock-weakened hand to seize the Box, got a good grip on it, and lifted himself up and through and out, right into the Other Zone.

. . .

Yesterday, the Newlands box had contained a wealth of informa-tional files once belonging to Uncle Li, Tuan's supposed father; files, voice clips, records, plus a miscellany of other evidence that would have been able to convict him of multiple crimes in any World Allied Court, should he make it to such a court without bribing off half the ships in the WAOF.

Now, the thin glass-like meter showed a progression of files that were entirely new—and still growing in number.

"There's more—the box just spontaneously generated more files," Tuan said, his voice an awed whisper. "I don't know who's doing it, and I don't know how, but—"

"Selroy," said Kez.

"What?"

"It sez Selroy," she said, pointing. "Sez *'allo* as well. Someone's playin' silly beggars wiv us as well as time an' space?"

Tuan looked down at the tiny display, and there it was. *Hello. This is Selroy. Please connect the Newlands Box to the Core.*

"Put it on the display," said Marx, rubbing a hand wearily across his face. "I can't read that."

Tuan did as he was told with a sinking feeling. He already thought he might understand more than he wanted to.

The message appeared on the *Upsydaisy*'s front panel, easier to read but no more palatable.

Hello. This is Selroy. Please connect the Newlands Box to the Core. It will need time to calibrate. If you wish to join this reality, please proceed to the co-ordinates below and observe a constant speed of—"

"I don't think this is from the person who undid the Fixed Points," Tuan said slowly. "I think it's from someone who's trying to help us fix them again."

"So long as it ain't a trap," muttered Kez. She looked as though she was still trying to shake off the stark fear she had experienced while observing the disintegrating timestream.

"I don't think so," Tuan said, the words tumbling over them-selves. "I think he's—I think he's trying to tell me how to—well, I've got a suspicion, but I'll need to think about it first."

"Ain't got real long to think about it," Kez reminded him. "We gotta figure out which Fixed Points were smashed and get 'em fixed again, don't we?"

"Which two did they unfix?" demanded Marx. "That's what we need to know."

"Yes," said Tuan, his mind moving very quickly. That was exactly the thing: as far as he could work out, there was only one way to find out for sure where a point of diversion had occurred to make two realities from one. He scanned the message one more time to assure himself that he was right in his surmises, and found that both Kez and Marx were staring at him when he finished.

"Go on, then," said Kez, encouragingly. "These messed up Fixed Points. Wot about 'em? Wot are we s'posed to do wiv this? 'Ow do we find out which ones need fixin'?"

"Fixed Points," repeated Tuan, to buy himself a little bit of time. "Well, we know that when Fixed Points are unfixed, the universe becomes unstable."

"We know that," said Kez. "Just listened to ourselves talkin' about it. 'Oo went round and undid 'em last time? So that we know what happens when they do?"

"No one," said Tuan, feeling rather cold. "No one has ever tried to do it before. This is *theoretical* knowledge: I don't think anyone thought that a person could be stupid enough to try and make the timeline deviate from what it's supposed to do."

"Well, someone 'as. Wot do we need to do, then?"

"First," Tuan said, a bright, sparkling enthusiasm settling over him, "We need to get into the other realities. We need to know which Fixed Points to refix. Then we have to come back and cement those points again."

"Listen, kid," said Marx. "It's not as though I don't trust you, but messing with alternate realities is a bit bigger than what we usually deal with, and I reckon you've never had to deal with them, either."

"Not in reality," Tuan said. "But in theory and in models—and he's basically *told* me what I need to know."

Kez blinked at him. "Oi, *where*? I ain't seen it!"

"Not directly, but he's given me the speed, position, and relative time that we need to reach, which means that if I can get us alongside our other selves in the other reality—I need to think about this."

Kez, grinning, allowed him to think: Marx, folding his arms and leaning against the bulkhead, did the same. Tuan thought for a very long time, his eyes wide and fascinated, before he finally said again, "He's given me the method and the calculations and even a bit of theory so that I think I can understand why it works, but the thing that really makes it work, the *one* thing he doesn't have, is you."

Kez grinned. "Irreplaceable, that's me! Figured there 'ad to be some way to make up for torchin' a whole planet; bein' a cog in a machine that's gunna save the universe is a pretty good make up, ain't it?"

"You didn't torch a whole planet," said Marx. "Someone who didn't want you around torched a whole planet. If anyone should be feeling like they owe the universe something, it's them."

To Tuan, he said, "You'd better make sure you do a good job of it. If we're going to be using Kez to power a machine—"

"Not to power it, exactly," said Tuan. "More like to open a doorway—or link up to another version of ourselves with a hawser line for just long enough for us to jump from this *Upsydaisy* into that *Upsydaisy*."

Marx gazed at him for some time before he said, "Hawser lines don't do real well when tethered ships are moving a bit too fast."

"We only need it for a fraction of an instant," Tuan said. "After that, there'll already be a hole punched through that reality. All I have to do is pull you back when we decide it's a good time."

"I vote yes," said Kez, to Marx. To Tuan, she said, "I vote for not dyin', too. 'F'you end up killin' me, I'm comin' back to haunt ya, Tuan Tuan."

Selroy floated there for a little while, amused to waft along in the grip of the same woolly feeling he had experienced with his tongue, this time softening sensation all over his body. It was difficult to feel worried about the patches of nothing he could see forming all across the Other Zone when everything was so muffled.

Selroy was aware that his train of thought, so shuffling and unconcerned, was dangerous. The disintegration of the universe in general had extended as far as the Other Zone, and he had no time to float aimlessly, categorising the sensations he was at present experiencing. Regretfully, he pulled his thoughts away from his physical feelings and turned them to what he needed to do next. First, he needed to know where he had to enter the timestream again.

He had never been able to move through time by himself, though in the Other Zone he could see the connections there to be made, but when it came to shifting, Selroy could shift in space with a pin-point accuracy not even achieved by personal portable shifters. He took pride in that, though he had never shared that particular talent with his co-workers at the Incursion Specialists. That, Selroy knew, was the quickest way into an Incursion Specialist-monitored cell. He had no interest in being on the inside of one of those cells: he quite disliked being on the outside of them, too, but given the choice between prisoner and prison warden, he much preferred the latter.

There wasn't much chance of advancing his research from behind prison bars, for one thing.

Selroy took a few moments longer to ensure that the current woolliness of his mind wasn't affecting his ability to utilise his talent, and slipped sideways again to the location in reality that had made everything in his universe wobble and disintegrate a little more with his knowledge of it.

Gravity took hold of his body at once, a relief and a sobering reminder at the same time. Relief, because it meant he had shifted himself to the exact place he wished to be; a sobering reminder because as he became aware of the gravity around him, so too, did his body.

Selroy's legs folded beneath him, sliding him gracefully if not gently to the floor, and he found himself looking up at everything somewhat dreamily.

"So this is the *Upsydaisy*," he mumbled , testing out his tongue. It had lost the woolly feeling, but unfortunately that loss had brought with it a deep and abiding pain that should have radiated from his shoulder but seemed merely to pulse in every part of him instead.

He'd managed to bring himself into some sort of recreation area: cool and cluttered, it would have looked a lot bigger than it did if it had been kept clean, but it wasn't terribly big to begin with. He'd expected the *Upsydaisy* to be bigger—or had he simply become used to the larger working quarters he'd had for so long now?

A chatter of sound pulled his attention away to his left, where a hatch cracked open, letting in light and sound.

"—an it ain't like Uncle Cheng's been real friendly to start wiv, anyway!" shouted a female voice. "I reckon we ought to go after 'im an' blow up 'is stupid liddle planet!"

"At least we've been able to see him!" came a faint yell. Male. "These Incursion Specialists are the ones that worry me!"

If Selroy had been able to feel any colder than he already felt, he would have gotten chills. They knew about the Incursion Specialists? How? And how much? Selroy had been certain that he had stayed in the shadows, and he was certain that Bell had done the same. No one should know about the Incursion Specialists, especially two recurring aberrations who had been causing their own incursions.

Selroy was still trying to figure that out when a small figure climbed into the rec room through the hatch and slapped on the lights. He saw flowered tights with a ladder in them, boots with a hole on the inner side of the right one where her foot must brush against the other a little too often, and a jumper that was far too big for the girl who wallowed in it.

Above the jumper was a skinny neck and a sharp, lean little face surrounded by black hair in a short bob and straight fringe. Two similarly black eyes stared accusingly at Selroy, and a voice as sharp as the face said, "You ain't s'posed to be 'ere."

Selroy eyed her uneasily as she got closer, and wondered if she would bite him if he told her to stay away from him.

"Oi," said the kid, coming closer and nudging him with the toe of her boot. "Wot are you doin' in 'ere?"

"Bleeding," Selroy said, with absolute truthfulness. "My regeneration doesn't seem to work very well right now. Perhaps it's because it's the end of the universe."

"Marx!" she yelled. "There's a bloke bleedin' in the rec room!"

As faintly as before, the male voice shouted, "If you've been putting animals in the rec room again, I'm going to boot you out the closest porthole!"

"Rude!" bawled the child, over her shoulder. "You better get yerself in 'ere, Marx!"

She turned her gaze on Selroy again, who thought to himself, *She's a very small aberration. What use can she be?*

"Rude!" said the kid again, surprising him into realising that he'd spoken aloud. Over her shoulder, she yelled once more, "*Marx*! There's a *bloke* bleedin' in the *rec room*! It ain't *animals*!"

She turned back to Selroy and prodded him with her boot again.

"Oi, Celery. Don't go to sleep just yet, all right? I'm Kez. Reckon you can get up?"

"My face feels numb," Selroy said. "It's very interesting. I don't really have time to explore this; I have to finish the Box."

Kez stared at him as though he was burbling, and perhaps he

was. At length she seemed to relent, and said, "If you ain't gunna try to get to the medipod, we might as well 'ave a bit of a talk, I s'pose. Marx might be able to lift ya in there, but ain't much good tryin' to do shifting right now."

"No, I wouldn't advise it," said Selroy, remembering the ruination of the Other Zone. "A bit messy in there right now with reality falling apart."

Her eyes sharpened on him. Kez said, very slowly, "'Zactly wot d'you mean by that, bucko?"

"Ready?" asked Kez.

Tuan was grateful to her: the words hadn't seemed to be able to make their way out of his throat. He opened his mouth to say yes, but said "No," instead.

"That makes two of us," said Marx. "Kid, if you keep kicking me in the back of the chair, I'm going to—"

Kez made an insulting sort of *pft* at him. "Wot you gunna do, old man?" she said, grinning a tough little grin that was the mirror-image of the one Marx was trying not to grin in the opposite direction.

"Kids," Marx said to Tuan. "Take in the feral ones, bring 'em up—"

"—kidnap, more like—"

"—give 'em every advantage in life—"

"—death threats, ya mean—"

"—and they still end up calling you *old man* instead of *dad*."

"Like you wouldn't leave me on Firteenth World if I did that!" scoffed Kez. "Oi. TuanTuan. We're ready."

"Yes," said Tuan, but he didn't seem to be able to move his fingers to start the entry sequence.

"You said you can get us back," Marx said, his voice horribly calm. It was even, Tuan thought, vaguely encouraging.

"I can," he said, but his voice was breathless. "I just have to invert the connection, and that should bring you right back here."

"Then wot you waitin' for?" demanded Kez. "We trust ya, TuanTuan. Push the button!"

"Actually it's a series of coordinates and connections that—"

"Push the button, kid," said Marx. "The Core is flashing purple, and I don't like doing sideways stuff when the Core is purple."

Tuan did as he was told, his chest tight and his heart in his mouth. He wanted to go with them, but if he did, there would be no one left here to pull on the ropes, so to speak, to get everyone back safely home.

Someone had to man the ropes. Tuan just wished it wasn't him. Then again, he was rather glad not to be punching holes in the universe personally.

The last sequence came too quickly. Tuan tapped the alpha-numeric series and hovered for a moment over the final button, catching Kez's mirrored black eyes. In their reflection he saw himself standing there, uncertain as always, and straightened his shoulders.

"Ready?" he asked, and was rather proud of the fact that his voice didn't tremble, though it was perhaps a touch higher than it usually was.

"See ya soon, TuanTuan," said Kez, and perhaps he'd been waiting for that one last acknowledgement, because as it came, Tuan touched the final number in the sequence, almost without realising it.

So light. So easy.

And they were gone.

"Reality is falling apart—" began Selroy, but she interrupted him.

"Not that," she said impatiently. "Already *seen* that! Wot you know about shiftin'?"

Selroy drew in a deep breath. "You're the one who shifts?

Not the man?"

"I shift pretty quickly when I'm needed," said a grey, dry voice from the hatch.

"Not through time and space," Selroy said. "How do you manage to be an aberration if you can't do that?"

Kez scowled at him. "You callin' me an aberration? Listen, mate, you got a lotta cheek for a bloke wot can't even get 'is feet under 'im."

"I don't need my feet under me," Selroy told her. "I just need a console and a Core connection. You'll need to make sure we keep a constant speed and direction for the next—"

Marx said, "You'll need to explain to me why I shouldn't heave you out the garbage hatch."

"No use doing that. I'll only come back in again. Are we moving at a regulated speed?"

"You already know too much," said Marx. "I'm not giving you any information you don't—you don't—"

He stuttered to a stop, in an almost automaton manner, and Selroy saw Kez sway in his peripheral, too. He watched Marx instead, wide-eyed to catch every detail, and saw the man blink twice, slowly. Kez said something that was more nonsense sound than actual words, and Marx's hand twitched, as if trying to force his body to respond to her.

Fascinating! thought Selroy, watching avidly. This—what he was seeing right now—was the process of two souls from another reality forcing their way into their corresponding bodies in this reality.

"How very interesting!" he burbled, as Marx drew in another deep, shuddering breath. "I always hoped I'd live to see the first visitors from another reality!"

Marx stared at him for a very long time; attempting, Selroy was rather certain, to find his way around the body in which he had found himself. It would be the same as his old body, of course, but it couldn't possibly be the same mentally. Whatever diversion had caused this reality to split from the original, it would have left different memories and experiences in its wake. Original Marx was trying to work his way around the memories and thought patterns of this reality's Marx.

At last, Marx said, "Who the flaming heck are you, and why are you on my ship?"

"I'm here to help." Selroy thought about that for a while, then added, "Peripherally, anyway. Actually, I just need somewhere to sit and work for a while. It'll be helpful to you, though."

Vaguely threatening, Marx said, "I don't like people appearing on my ship whenever they feel like it."

"It's not your ship." Selroy caught the black, glittering gaze of Kez, who had awoken with eyes even deeper and more piercing than before, and tried not to shudder.

"Told ya," said Kez, grinning at Marx, and then turning that grin on Selroy, who wished she wouldn't. "Ain't yore ship, old man."

Marx crossed his arms. "I'd shoot you, but it looks like someone's already taken care of it. Was it me?"

"No," said Selroy. "It was someone at the Incursion Specialists who was trying to stop me from getting to you. They're WAOF, you'll run into them later, I should think, if everything comes out properly. How was your trip?"

"You know a lot more than I like you knowing," said the other man, in a conversational sort of way that might have fooled Selroy if he hadn't been familiar with the very hard gleam in Marx's eyes. He had once seen that gleam before—from a much older version of this same man, if he wasn't mistaken.

"I said that to you," he said, in wonder. "Well, you haven't heard it yet, but you will. I've already met a much older version of you—when I didn't know it was you. You're the one who got me into the research that—you're the one who let me know I'm not alone."

"Very heart-warming," said Marx. "But that doesn't explain why you're *here*, on my *ship*, and I'm only going to excuse blood-loss for a little bit longer before I start hitting you."

"You've come a long way to start hitting people," Selroy said. "And it won't do you any good, anyway. If you let me get to work, you might just be able to save your own version of reality. You'll have to take the box back with you, of course."

Kez's sharp eyes fastened on the Newlands Box and she gave vent to a gleeful chuckle deep in her throat that would have curdled Selroy's blood had his blood been in any condition to curdle.

"Oi, Marx," she said. "This mucker 'as the Newlands Box!"

"Wonderful!" said Selroy. "So it got to you, then! You know the universe is falling apart and you've come to find the point of divergence to fix it in your reality."

"This mucker's *Selroy*," Kez said, with the wrathful surprise of someone who comes face-to-face with a stranger in the mess hall, only to find out that this same stranger is the one who spat in their coffee. She looked Selroy up and down in wary distrust, and added, "Surprised they don't call you Celery."

"The other version of you did," he offered, and Marx gave a short crack of laughter.

When Selroy looked at him, however, the man was entirely sober.

"Let me get this straight," said Marx. His tone was conversational, but Selroy still felt the distinct threat to it. "The universe is falling apart—"

"Already knew that," Kez muttered. She was frowning, and he wondered if she was beginning to access the other Kez's recent memories of him. "Saw the mess."

"And you're the one who sent us the box loaded with all the instructions on how to get here."

"I input the instructions," said Selroy, "but I rather fancy you're the ones who sent the box to yourselves. I can move in space, but not time, and I certainly can't thin the walls of existence to such a point that it's possible to push something through. I'm just here to finish the box so that you can send it. It's hard enough linking it with the right places in the Core, let alone in the original reality, so some of the information might not go through just exactly right. You'll have to be careful for that when you get back."

"How do you know us?" asked Marx, after a brief pause in which Selroy had expected him to ask about the ability he had just mentioned.

It wasn't a wrong question; it was perhaps even pertinent. But Selroy still felt dizzy, although he could also feel his skin cells moulding themselves around the edges of his wound, and it seemed good to preserve energy.

He said, "I have enough energy to either program the box or answer your questions about your future and my past. Which would you rather me do?"

"The box," Marx said, rather grimly. Selroy was pleased to note that he said it without hesitation, however. "But we'll be watching you. What do you need?"

"Time," said Selroy. "Concentration. Access to the Core. Maybe a blood transfusion later."

"Off to the bridge, then," said Marx.

Selroy didn't expect the move to be easy, but he wasn't quite prepared for the amount of pain the hole in his shoulder caused him. Fortunately, the further pain also seemed to clear his mind, and even if it didn't abate once Marx had dumped him in a bucket-chair by the main console in the tiny bridge, neither did his clarity of mind.

"I'll get the blood," offered Kez, and disappeared.

Marx, in an even friendlier tone than before, said, "If you do anything stupid in the Core, I'll shoot another hole in you, savvy?"

"Two holes; got it," said Selroy, his mind already on the job.

Someone laughed, soft and genuinely amused, but Selroy catalogued that to consider later, when he could concentrate on words and meanings again. He was so close to finishing the box: he just needed to pre-program it with all the right loose ends so that it connected with the original version of the Core when it got to the original reality.

As he worked, someone attached a bag of simu-blood to his arm, and the sudden rush of blood-substitute and oxygen sent a prickling wave of awareness over him.

"Power up!" said Selroy, gurgling to himself.

"Reckon this bloke's a bit daft," opined someone.

"He's all right," said the male voice. "It's just the oxygen rush."

Selroy ignored both the voices, but the burble of conversation continued, and he allowed it to wash over him as he worked, cataloguing it for later listening, too.

"So we're waitin' for him to finish the box so we can send it back to ourselves?"

"Looks like it."

"Well, I'm gunna look for TuanTuan in the Core. I don't like this bloke."

"Go for it. While you're at it, see if you can find out where this reality split from ours, why don't you?"

"You bein' sarcastic?"

"Yeah. Listen, kid; if your pet lieutenant isn't here, it's probably because—"

"Wot?"

"Never mind. Shove over; we'll see what we can find in the Core. It's not like we know what we're looking for but—"

"Yeah, we do."

"Since when?"

"Well, I memorised our Fixed Points. Ain't memorised all the Fixed Points in the universe, but—"

"You what?"

"Memorised 'em."

"Why would you—?"

"Dunno, seemed like a good idea. An' they're *ours*: wot else was I s'posed to do? Anyway, we just gotta look in the Core an' see wot ones ain't listed, right? It's a start, right?"

"Kid, I've wronged you."

"Yeah, wouldn't be the first time."

"Kid."

"Yeah?"

"Shut up and get looking."

There was silence for some time, but all too soon, the mutter of voices began again.

"Oi. Looks like—this version's a mess 'cos this version of us tried to go back an' fix a Fixed Point an' it didn't go real well."

"We already knew that, kid."

"Yeah, but now I *seen* it. I ain't trustin' no voice even if it *is* mine."

"Glad to hear it," said Marx's voice. And then, to Selroy's relief, he added, "Less talk, more work, kid."

Tuan expected to see what he usually saw when Kez did her shifts in time and space: Kez there, and then Kez not there. Kez and Marx, then no Kez and Marx. He didn't expect to see their eyes dull and their heads drop, the life utterly and completely removed from them in an instant.

For one horrible moment, Tuan panicked and nearly punched the button that would end the sequence and bring them back; then he realised that they were both still breathing, and that although their eyes were lifeless, their bodies were not.

He slid to the floor, legs weak and trembling, and concentrated on breathing for quite some minutes before he remembered that he had to be keeping a watch on time. Keeping a watch on time: now there was a joke for Kez when she came back.

Tuan snuffled a laugh into his arm, his voice as shaky as his legs, and reran his calculations on the small, portable interface he had taken to the floor with him. There would be some difference to the degradation of this reality and that to which Kez and Marx had gone, but so long as he kept a steady pace here with the *Upsydaisy* and replicated everything else as best he could, he could keep the connection between them—that door, or perhaps crawlspace, between realities—open. When it looked like it would become too unsteady for safety, he would pull Kez and Marx back straight away. He hoped they were busy finding out where the differences lie, because Tuan had a very good idea that they had only one chance to make this right. He had already seen the disintegration that followed Kez and Marx's shift into the other reality: small, visible pieces missing from the *Upsydaisy* that shouldn't have disintegrated so soon. It would be the same, or perhaps worse, in the other reality, and Tuan was very well aware that they were on limited time.

The calculations came out again correctly, which steadied Tuan's legs enough to allow him to stand up and check Marx and Kez properly. As he had already seen, they were still breathing, and when he went to fetch two of the one-use health-check packs from the storage space beneath the medipod, the results were enough to cheer him. They were alive and well; merely unconscious, if the health-check packs were to be believed. Tuan didn't quite believe them, but he was comforted despite that.

He had made a mistake in supposing that their entire bodies would go into the other dimension, but now that he knew that, he was sure he could refine his process for next time. If, he thought uneasily, looking around at the few, tiny missing pieces of reality, there was enough time to do anything about it when they came back.

And if, he thought, tugging even more uneasily at his hair and trying to stop himself from starting the sequence to pull them back home, they came back at all.

"Wot now?" demanded Kez. "Once we know exactly when an' where to push the Box through, it's tied up all nice and tidy, ain't it?"

Selroy, who was feeling bright and light and satisfied, said,

"That's it. What you do with it in your reality is up to you. Did you find your point of division?"

"The Fixed Points what were messed wiv? Yeah. Two of 'em, like you said; both missing in this reality—both of 'em ones that are attached to us."

"Very well. Then we'd best begin."

"We need to think about how we're going to get out of here, first," said Marx, rather grimly. "We should have been snapped back into the other reality a few minutes ago, if I'm any judge of how long we've been here."

"You can't get back to your reality from here," Selroy said, in surprise. "And certainly not until we finish sending the Box through."

Marx looked grimmer. "I was beginning to suspect that. We expected to come here bodily, for a start. We were also supposed to snap back to our own reality when our science-man broke the connection with this reality a few minutes ago."

"That won't work," Selroy told them, frowning. Whoever their science man was, he'd accomplished something that Selroy himself hadn't—it was just that he hadn't quite managed to do it correctly. The theory was sound, but Selroy was rather sure that no one had taken into account the increasing speed of decomposition of this universe due to the arrival of Kez and Marx. "We're no longer moving at the same speed as the other universe, so to speak; your arrival threw that off. The connection would have broken as soon as you arrived. You'd have to go back further in time where everything is a bit better aligned."

"And our science man won't be here to help us, either," Marx said, with increasing grimness. "He's apparently doing other things."

"Your science man? No, no, don't tell me," Selroy added.

"Weren't *gunna* tell ya!" Kez said resentfully. "He ain't around, anyway! You lot flamin' messed 'is life up for 'im."

"You can't expect everything to be the same here," he reminded her. "Anyway, don't tell me things I don't need to know.

If I don't know, there's less chance that anyone else will know. The less anyone knows about what we're about to do, the more likely it'll come off safely. The Core already collects too much information."

Kez stared at him, her eyes glassy. "'Ow are we gunna get back to our reality if our science man ain't 'ere to 'elp us an' our line snapped?"

"I can't do anything about it," said Selroy simply. "The connection he had with you is gone; we're decomposing far too quickly, now."

"Wot if we tried to get back through where we've made reality thinner? Take the box through ourselves?"

"There would already be too many versions of you in that time and place," Selroy told her. "You'd risk making another Fixed Point *or* another tear in your reality. To fix your reality, you have to give up on getting back and focus on just pushing the box through. That's the important thing."

"What's the good of trying to send that back, if we can't get back with it?" asked Marx, leaning against the bulkhead as if to gain strength, one clenched fist tapping lightly against it. He nodded at the Newlands Box. "How will it help to have that there? We'll just end up coming here again, looking for it in this reality."

"It's a tiny core," said Selroy. "And now it's updated with everything you'll need, in all aspects of time and reality. Or it will be, once you get it back through to your reality. Your younger selves will have access to it, too: you'll be able to save the original reality."

"Rude," said Kez. "After us doin' all the work to get 'ere, the least you could do is send it over for us."

"Not possible," Selroy said. "But with your gift—"

"There you go, knowin' stuff you shouldn't know again," she pointed out.

"You're lucky I know what I know," he told her. "That specific place that's a bit thinner—"

The two of them exchanged a look, and he wondered if they were thinking of their *science man*, who had very nearly gotten right what even Selroy was only just beginning to understand.

"Yeah," said Kez. "A place where we stole the box about three times, yeah? The Core kept sayin' we were gunna steal it again. Guess it was right."

Marx shot a thoughtful look at him. "It'll definitely go through to all the realities?"

"Reality is just thin enough there that someone who can access the Other Zone can push it through to the original. Maybe to the others."

"Ain't no *maybe* about it," Kez said. "We're here. We already done it."

"Ye-es," said Selroy doubtfully, who understood a good deal more about the general squishiness and unreliability of reality than she did. "At any rate, we'd best try; and soon."

"'Ang on," said Kez, her eyes hard and glittering. "Gotta leave ourselves a message: if we ain't gettin' back no matter what we do, we'd be makin' sure we fix up our reality. Maybe—maybe that'll change things up a bit."

"A voice message," Marx said, as if in agreement, meeting Kez's glittering eyes.

"That will take too long," protested Selroy, but he knew he had already lost that battle. "All right, but be quick! We still have to drop the box in the right time and place and hope it goes through to all realities. We need to concentrate on the important things."

Kez grinned at him; a tough, fierce little thing that made Selroy aware that she was probably quite used to paring down to the important things. "Don't you worry, bucko," she said. "This is one of the important things."

Tuan had to physically restrain himself from activating the sequence that would bring Kez and Marx home. It was early: far too early.

To prevent himself starting the sequence too early and pulling them back before they got the information they needed, Tuan put all of his files in order, pulling information from the Core as quickly as he could before it was deteriorated beyond repair.

All he would need to do when Kez and Marx got back was refine his theory on accessing other realities, and update the box with all of the tidied files and the Fixed Points that needed to be addressed. There were a few possible incursions in the Core that made him think they would have to venture into another reality at some stage to find the source of another Unfixed Point, so Tuan listed those as well, worried to note that the decay in the Core was now obvious, as was the decomposition here and there around the bridge of the *Upsydaisy*.

By the time he was done with his sequencing, Tuan had almost forgotten to look at his timer.

Almost.

He looked again when there were only two minutes to go— two minutes that felt like two hours. Tuan waited for those two minutes to drag by, then, hardly able to breathe in his eagerness, he started the home-bound sequence.

No connection, said the message on the screen of his portable interface. He entered the sequence again, faster, and the message disappeared for a moment, only to reappear, this time blinking.

No connection.

Tuan swayed where he stood; fell back against the bulkhead and retched, again and again. He'd been wrong. He'd been so wrong. It wasn't working. And with another stab of nausea, he understood why. This reality and the one in which Kez and Marx were trapped were beginning to move at different speeds of decomposition.

It was already too late to bring them back.

. . .

The bulkhead against which Marx leaned was the first thing to disappear.

"That's torn it," he said. "C'mmere, kid."

"Oo-er! Marx, lookit—! Marx!"

An edge of floral skirt that had fluttered a moment ago now didn't exist; eating into Kez's leg, that disintegration moved at an observable pace.

"It's okay, kid," said Marx, drawing her close. "I got you. Close your eyes. It's okay."

Selroy snapped the Newlands Box shut as Kez said, "Ain't gunna close my eyes. Ain't got the time."

"Now," said Selroy. He'd already left it too long in order to record that one last message, and so had Kez and Marx. "You have to go and put the box where it needs to go, *now*."

"Flaming heck," Marx said softly, looking down his swiftly crumbling arm.

"Better go now, eh?" said Kez, but she wasn't looking at Selroy. She was still looking up at Marx, her free hand gripping tight to his whole arm.

"Yes," Selroy said anyway. "You're going to—"

Kez's voice was short, and far too old for her apparent years. "Fall apart? Yeah, got it."

"I mean that you've got one chance," said Selroy. "Into the Other Zone and out again with the box at exactly the right place and time. There'll be nothing left of you by the time you get back into the timestream, but the box will make it."

"Got it," she said. She laughed a bit, and said, "It's a flamin' crock, this. Didn't even get to say goodbye to—"

"I've got you, kid," said Marx. "We'll go together."

She didn't argue. Selroy wasn't sure if that was because she knew it was too late for Marx as well, or if she just wanted him with her.

Before they could go, he said to Marx, "It's not the Incursion Specialists, you know. They're ambitious, not insane; they know the risks of this sort of thing. Your version of the Holstrom

Institute might have a bit to tell you: an extinct timeline from there was brought back a few months ago, relatively speaking. Find out who brought Marcus Solomon back and you'll have your man."

"Told ya," said Kez to Marx, her chin wobbling and her eyes black and pebbly. "Didn't I?"

"Heard you the first time, kid," the other man said. "Told you I'd deal with it, didn't I?"

It shouldn't have sounded particularly tough, coming from a man the size of Marx, but Selroy felt a chill seep over him that might not be just his discomposing body.

It seemed to cheer Kez up, however, because she laughed again, this time gruffly, and said, "You ready, old man?"

"Always," said Marx, and they were gone.

With them went most of Selroy's right arm and a good portion of the console in front of him. Perhaps, thought Selroy to himself, as his foot began to disintegrate; perhaps he should have told them that their spirits would go back to their own timeline once the pieces of the host bodies in his reality fully disassociated.

They hadn't asked about that, but people never did ask the right things.

Never mind, thought Selroy rather dreamily, for falling to pieces didn't hurt, but it made it hard for thoughts to form in the spaces between his molecules.

He was rather sure they'd found that out for themselves by now, anyway.

It was too long. Tuan paced the short distance across the *Upsy-daisy*'s bridge, back and forth, clutching his hands around his neck in a frantic attempt at self-comfort, his forearms pressing against his ears.

They'd been gone *too long* and he couldn't get them back. Why had he said he knew what he was doing? Why had he let them trust him? Kez was in an alternate reality, and he already knew she would die because he had *heard* it. Why had he thought so well of himself to think that he could protect them when he couldn't even go along with them?

Tuan tried to stop the tears, but they fell anyway, warm and fast and hopeless. When there was nothing else to do—no other idea how to reach through into the next reality and drag Kez back—he lifted her out of the seat and sat there himself, hugging her to his chest.

Waxy and still, she didn't move until she suddenly *did*, breaking his grip around her and sitting bolt upright to grasp Tuan by the fluffy neck of his jumper.

"You better be you, TuanTuan," she said. "Or I'm gunna punch ya."

Tuan took in a deep, sobbing breath, and buried his face in her neck. "You're back!"

"S'all right," said Kez, even though her hands still gripped the simu-wool. "'S'all right, TuanTuan. We're back. You did good."

"You're back," he said again, flushed and dizzy. He knew that Kez was comforting him when he should be comforting her, and if he'd been able to think about it properly, it probably would have occurred to him that it was the first time she had really done so. But right now it was too hard to think about anything except the fact that Kez was alive, was here—was safe.

"Flaming heck," Marx said, rather thickly. "That was unpleasant. Is that going to happen every time?"

"I don't know," Tuan said, with another shuddering breath. That one seemed to steady him; or perhaps it was simply the warmth of Kez in his lap, clinging to his shoulders and muttering distinctly discomforting things in a comforting tone. "I don't—I don't even know what happened. I tried to bring you back, but it didn't work."

"We know," said Marx. "We died over there; made it back

here all right, though. Could have been worse. *What* did you say, kid?"

Kez, who had been crooning things like, *Don't worry Tuan-Tuan, you're all right TuanTuan, we're gunna go an' get that bloke's other fingerbone and set fire to that liddle garden, so you better be all right, eh, TuanTuan*—looked up and glared at him.

"Wasn't talkin' to you," she said. Up to four years ago, she would probably have told him to mind his own business, so Tuan supposed that was forward motion. "I'm talkin' to TuanTuan. Can't you see 'e needs to 'ave a bit of a rest?"

"We don't have time for a rest," said Tuan, rather thankfully. He already had one fingerbone ring and he wasn't sure he wanted that one. He certainly didn't want another. "The universe is still falling apart, and I don't yet know enough to fix it."

"Selroy knows," said Kez. "Well, the bit that you don't know, he knew. Didn't seem to know what you know, though; you weren't wiv us, over there."

Tuan, who had been all too aware of that fact since listening to the box, wrapped his arms tightly around her thin torso again.

Marx stretched himself to his full height, which wasn't particularly high, and gave a satisfied groan when a few pops sounded. "What *do* you know?"

"I know the bad news," said Tuan. Despite that bad news, he felt remarkably content with his arms around Kez and his chin resting on her head. Even if he was dead in that other reality, he was gloriously alive here. "We can't do this again—pushing through to another reality, I mean. Not this version of us—at this age. You didn't repair the Fixed Point from that side, and it sped up the rate of decomposition on this side just by going there."

"That's all right," Kez said. "Selroy reckoned that this thing 'ere updates itself in time and space like the Core does. We can send it to ourselves in a nice, tidy part of the universe where there ain't a lot of damage yet. I got two Fixed Points we need to sort out to start wiv: saw 'em in the Core over there."

"Hopefully we can do something about them before someone breaks another," Tuan said.

"Don't worry," said Marx, with a hard grin. "We'll be doing something about that, too. We've got a pretty good idea who it is, now. It's about time that Time Corp and the WAOF knew about it, too."

"Think they'll care?" Kez asked, rather sceptically. "Reckon they're pretty good friends wiv Uncle Cheng, and he's the only one wot'd have the money and drive to bring back Marcus."

"The universe is falling apart. I reckon they'll care."

"Good point," said Kez. "Oi, pull up the Core, Marx."

"What am I, your slave?"

But Marx opened the Core interface anyway, and Kez, apparently happy to remain with Tuan, jerked her chin at the list of Fixed Points. "That one," she said. "An' that one. Gotta get those sorted out first. Whatever else they try after that—or before that—at least we'll get those ones done. Sorta stabilise things a bit."

"That one'll be tricky," Marx said, indicating the first. "*We* can't do it—even past us can't do it: we were all there for that one. We're going to need help."

Tuan, remembering the message in the Newlands Box, suggested, "The sort of help that goes around with Time Corp and seems to be inclined to assist you every now and then?"

Kez laughed gleefully. "Yep."

"I've got an idea that now would be a good time to find out exactly how Arabella was hired, and who did it," said Marx, more thoughtfully. "Hire her ourselves if no one else looks like they're doing it."

"Who else *would* do it?" said Tuan. "I mean, really?"

"Wot, you reckon we're the ones 'oo hired her in the first place?" demanded Kez, grinning.

"Looks like it," said Marx, shrugging; but he was grinning, too.

Tuan had often wondered exactly how much Arabella knew

about the people she called *her employers*: he was quite certain now that those employers were himself, Kez, and Marx.

"I'll figure out a timeline," he said, with a fizz of hope to his heart. "You said this thing updates across all timelines? What if I put in a list of things that we know need to be done, along with all the information we have on how to do it? Make sure the box is opened in places where there isn't as much fallout? Then we'd all be working on it at once; all the iterations of us. Make sure we tell ourselves to tick things off as we do them?"

Marx gazed at him for a very long time, and Tuan felt his hopes fall. He'd done too much wrong; he'd wanted a chance to prove himself, and he'd failed miserably. No doubt Marx was thinking about throwing him back on the *TCS Slider* as soon as he could.

To his surprise, Marx said, "Do it. I can play with the Core just enough to get us into trouble, but you can make patterns with it. We'll move out as soon as you've updated everything. We'll need to get that box where it needs to go."

"Reckon we already did," interrupted Kez. "Just gotta sorta draw attention to it, like. In the right place and time."

"But first," continued Marx, "we need to figure out a way to convince Arabella to work for us."

"Pft," Kez said dismissively. "That's the easy bit."

"Not if we don't want people to know about it. If she's connected to us, Uncle Cheng will be able to trace us through her, and there goes our chance of being able to fix our problems using her."

"Pft," said Kez again. "All we gotta do is keep playin' wiv Golden Boy. Bells'll go anywhere for 'im, even if she won't let 'im hurt us."

"Oh!" said Tuan, who had been processing the to-do list on the Box while he waited for the Core to show up the most whole points in their timeline. "That one just vanished."

They both stared at him. "The one for corrupting Arabella?" asked Marx. "Good grief!"

"One of the possible infractions just vanished, too," Tuan said in awe. He checked the position of the change, and said, "Oh! That one matches up with one of the areas of our timeline where there's the least damage!"

"We'd better get to work sending the box there, then," Marx said. "Without letting our past selves see our present selves, if we can possibly help it."

"I might be able to help with that," said Tuan, slapping the Box shut. He had finished transferring all his data to it; there was nothing else he could put into it, and it was unnerving to see files disappearing before his eyes in a way that it wasn't when he saw it happening in the Core. "You remember that Temporary Sideways Engine I've been working on?"

"Not a clue," said Kez, quite cheerfully, taking the box from him.

Tuan protested, "I told you about it!"

"Don't mean I know what you're talkin' about," she pointed out. "You're too clever for your own good, TuanTuan. I ain't. Just tell me wot you're gunna do wiv it, yeah?"

Tuan sighed faintly, but said, "All right: give the box back to me. If I calculate it at just the right moment, I can put the box outside our hatch here in the *Upsydaisy*, and at the same time push it to a past iteration of you and Marx at just the right moment to be able to do what needs to be done with that possible incursion I told you about."

"Will we know how to fix the other broken points?" asked Marx. "What about the problem of us not being able to get back from other realities?"

"They already fixed it," Tuan said, but he couldn't repress a shiver. "I don't know how the younger versions of us figure it out, but we must do: they've already updated it in the box."

"Oh well," said Marx, shrugging. "Might as well nearly die in the past as well as now. Go for it."

"'Ang on," Kez said, her eyes glittering. "Gotta write a note first; that's polite, ain't it. *Kez woz 'ere*. That should do it!"

"Oi," said Kez irritably. "Someone shoved a note under the 'atch."

That wasn't all they'd shoved under the hatch: Kez had nearly stubbed her toe on a small box.

Marx didn't turn around from the console, which was more irritating. Kez didn't like to be ignored.

He said, "If you've been bringing stray animals into the *Upsydaisy* again, I'm going to punt you out the closest port hole."

"Ain't that," she told him, gingerly poking at the tiny parcel with the toe of her boot. "Look! It's a note and a liddle present and it was sittin' right by the 'atch when I got in 'ere. Didn't you see it when you come in?"

"What is it?"

"It's that box. Wiv a note, like I said."

"What's it say?"

There was a silence while Kez scowled at the note and tried to make the squiggles make sense. When they did, she said laboriously, "Sez it's from us."

That made Marx look up sharply, much to her glee. "What?"

"Sez it's from us," Kez repeated, more loudly. She shoved the box and note at him. "I can read, ya know."

Marx took the box from her, and she saw his brows rise at

the inscription on the top of the box. She hadn't been able to read that; it was a Seventh World phrase. Kez could speak, but not read, Seventh World language.

"Who sends paper notes these days?" he asked. He frowned at the note, and Kez grinned a bit, because she had already seen the bit at the bottom that he must have just seen. It said *kez woz 'ere*, just like the small chicken-scratch beneath the *Upsydaisy*'s console that she hadn't made yet but would one day, even though it was already there.

"Kid," he said, and there was a vague threat to his voice, "have you been playing silly beggars with the chronomatrix again?"

"Wasn't me!" Kez said indignantly. "Just gave it a bit of a bash wiv me spanner—"

"*My* spanner."

"—*our* spanner, when it got stuck, like."

"Have you been playing silly beggars with the ship's parts again, then?"

"That wasn't me either!" complained Kez. "It was that beastie! Ain't my fault the loo didn't come back for days afterward!"

Marx shot a rather grim look in her direction, but he opened the box. There was a very faint chirp of noise, then the *Upsydaisy*'s console screen flickered and began to run with Universal Script. Marx slammed the lid shut and the script paused, but didn't vanish.

"Coo!" said Kez, highly impressed. "Didn't know it could do that! Oi, Marx."

"What?"

"Wot's a *Selroy*?"

OUT OF ORDER

IT WAS NEARLY ELEVEN IN THE MORNING, AND DIRECTOR BELL had been going to the toilet non-stop since he woke up. Fortunately for the dignified image he preferred to present to his men, it was Director Bell's day off: he could, theoretically, retire to the toilet as often as he chose, within the comfort of his own quarters.

Unfortunately for Director Bell, his wife was afflicted with the same issue—no doubt the result of their late night foray into the interworld market yesterday, when they had eaten a very good Tamoan curry that had turned out to have an unfortunate and unforeseen effect—and she was currently occupying the toilet in their quarters. That left him the open toilets a few steps down the hallway from his door, which would have been all well and good had one of them not had an *out of order* sign hanging from the door when he arrived. Since there were only two toilets and the other was occupied, it had left Director Bell to wait and sweat until the staff member emerged and gave it up.

He had called for it to be fixed straight away; great was his annoyance, therefore, upon returning a little while later, to find the pernicious sign still in evidence.

Director Bell, trying to remember that his expectations of what was reasonable and the cleaning staff's expectations were at this time radically different, did not immediately call again. It wasn't until he had returned to the toilets twice more that he put in another call.

There was a momentary silence on the other end of the comms, then the cleaning staff said, "Yeah. We'll get right on that," and ended the communication. Bell wondered if it was just the excruciating agony in his bowels that made the staff member's voice sound so offensively blasé, or if the man had meant to be rude. Bell was quietly proud of the fact that he didn't throw his weight around, despite being one of the highest-ranking personnel at the Incursion Specialists; today, however, he had a sharp urge to contact the staff again and insist, in no uncertain terms, that they do as they were told with a minimum of cheek and a maximum of expediency.

Instead, he was forced to duck back into the second toilet again, preventing any kind of call out for the next fifteen minutes. When he at last emerged again to wash his hands and hover nervously around the door, unwilling to move too far away from safety, his comm buzzed once again.

Hoping for good news, Director Bell said, "Yes?"

"Good morning, sir!" said his lieutenant's voice, far too cheerfully.

"What is it, Lieutenant?"

The director didn't intend for his voice to be quite so annoyed, but he was finding it wasn't so easy to moderate his tones at the present.

"Sorry, sir," said the lieutenant. "Only you asked me to let you know whenever Selroy gets information on those two aberrations that turn up in the system every now and then, and—"

"Kez and Marx are back again?"

"Yes sir. The system had glitched, if you remember—"

"I do," Director Bell said, rather grimly, and this time his grimness had more to do with Kez and Marx than it did his current situation. "It's back to normal, then? The Core? Our readings?"

There was a brief hesitation before his lieutenant said, "Yee-es. That is, Selroy seems to think there are more Fixed Points than there ought to be, and the Core is still a bit unsure about them, too. But by and large, we're back where we think we ought to be."

"And Kez and Marx have made another appearance. I see. Weren't we able to clock them in time to make a capture attempt?"

"No sir, I'm sorry. We've just managed to catch their wake."

"Why wasn't it mapped? We have a good idea of their movements and their contacts by now, don't we? And we've been able to predict how they'll react to a range of different situations and stimuli. Are they really that good? I hadn't thought so."

"It's not that they're so good, exactly," the lieutenant said. "In my opinion."

"What *is* your opinion?" Bell forced himself to ask. A suspicious cramping had begun in his lower stomach once again. He would have liked to let the conversation go altogether and get back to the business at hand, but his lieutenant often had surprisingly deep insight and was worth listening to.

"Well, sir, they're bright and determined and really very sneaky, but if it was just that, we could map them and eventually catch them. We've been mapping them since they popped up in the system and new Fixed Points began to come out in the first place; but no matter what we do, we don't seem to be able to catch them. They always duck just as we dodge, or charge off sideways when we're making a bull-run for it."

Bell leaned against the wall and mopped sweat from his brow. "You mean they're unexpected."

"Yes, sir. But it's more than being unexpected; they've made a guerrilla art form out of it! They don't do things for the sake of being unexpected—they just go off on tangents that have no rhyme or reason, even when it comes to their established patterns. Sir, they blew up a transporter for apparently the sheer fun of it, and exposed a major drug operation just because they *didn't get a spork in their tuckbox*. We can't map that!"

"You're saying they didn't go out to expose the drug running?"

"No sir. It was a pure accident. They were after a spork and ran into some lollymen."

Bell drew in a deep breath. "What kind of spork? Was there anything special about it?"

"Just a reconstituted spork, sir. Nothing special about it except that it wasn't where they wanted it to be and they were annoyed about that."

"But that's ridiculous!"

"Yes, sir."

There was a moment of silence where Director Bell crouched over a little further and both hoped for and dreaded the continuation of the briefing.

A moment later, his lieutenant said diffidently, "I also suspect they've got help from within Time Corp."

Director Bell frowned. "Not that captain they're always trying to corrupt? Mikkel of the Time Corp? We sent someone in to keep an eye on that."

"No, sir. As far as we can tell, Captain Mikkel is firmly on our and Time Corp's side: those two have managed to map *him* out and use him as a piece in their game."

"They shouldn't be able to map out *anyone*," Bell said in exasperation. "What are they using for their computations, do you think? I've heard a suggestion that they've got a Time Corp craft."

"I wouldn't put it past them, sir."

Bell came to an obvious realisation. "But just having a Time Corp craft wouldn't be enough; if what you're suggesting is true, it would mean they've got Core access as well!"

"Yes, sir. I've been having a word with Selroy, and he thinks the same."

"Prepare a report," said Director Bell, with finality. "I'll have to take a look at this when I'm back on the bridge. No—send it to me as soon as it's done. I want to know the worst. Include your suspicions."

His comm chittered as the connection dropped. Bell attended to his increasingly urgent business and afterward returned rather weakly to his own quarters, where he tapped on the bathroom door to make sure his wife was still conscious and discovered her hearty enough to inform him in gorgon accents that if he ever thought to take her to the interworld markets again she would happily gut herself first and get the thing over with.

She must be feeling better, then, thought Bell, settling down rather gingerly on the couch. He was feeling a little better himself, so he ordered a pot of thin soup to be brought to the suite, and when it arrived, he gamely consumed a good half of it.

That turned out to be a mistake that sent him back to the toilets outside within five minutes of ingesting the stuff. Stumbling across the tiled floor, Bell bit back a groan at the sight of the *Out of Order* sign still in evidence, and nearly sank to his knees when his horrified gaze fell on the *occupied* sigil that decorated the door of the second toilet.

Director Bell tapped on the door with well-mannered desperation.

"Sorry," said a young female voice. "This one's taken."

It was unlikely, thought Bell, that he would make it to the next nearest toilet in time. He made the executive decision to ignore the *out of order* sign and pushed his way into the cubicle, feeling the weakness in his legs increase.

Even if the toilet was out of order, it should be partially usable. If it couldn't flush, it would at least save him from disgracing himself on the way to seek other shelter. Sweating, Bell pushed the button to access the toilet.

He wasn't prepared for the floor to fall away, dropping him into a tunnel that was sloped and slippery with no chance of finding purchase. Something shut above him as he fell, and he had time only for a gulp of dismay before the speed of his descent sent him tumbling out of the bottom of that tunnel and into a cool, haphazardly lit area that was distinctly softer than he expected it to be.

By the time he rolled to a stop, Bell had lost feeling from the waist down, though whether or not that was a good thing was yet to be seen.

"What the *blistering blazes* is this?" he groaned, crouching in on himself and grateful for the lack of initial squishiness. He was pleased to find that when he uncurled himself and staggered to his feet, his legs were capable of bearing him, though there was still a worrying lack of feeling to them.

Bell turned, trying to figure out what had happened and what fresh distress he had found himself in, and found himself suddenly face to stomach with a small girl in a jumper by far too large and armoured leggings that had a ladder in them.

"Oi," said the kid indignantly. "You ain't s'posed to be in 'ere! Can't you read? Sez it's not for use!"

"It says *out of order*," said Bell, vaguely grasping that she was speaking of the sign on the toilet above. "Can't *you* read?"

Those black eyes grew hard and glittery. "Ain't none of your business, is it?"

Director Bell came to three conclusions very rapidly.

One: this was not the child of any of the Facility's staff. The children of his staff were tidy, if inclined to be arrogant, and none of them would have treated him with this kind of disrespect, even while he was out of uniform.

Two: This child, small and dark and rage-filled, must be Kez, though how and why she had made it into the bowels of the Incursion Specialists' base of operations was still an unsolved puzzle.

Three: While he had been distracted by conversation with the repellent child, a grey shadow had appeared at his back, fluttering with a movement that teased his peripheral and split open his head.

Consciousness came painfully, but the pain wasn't where Director Bell expected it to be. His stomach no longer felt like a cross between a furnace and a pin-cushion for red-hot pins, but his head had taken over that function instead.

"'Allo," said a cheerful voice. "Looks like 'e's comin' round!"

Director Bell couldn't quite remember to whom that voice belonged, but he was instinctively aware that he disliked it. He opened his eyes, groaning, and wished the room wouldn't swing around him when he tried to sit up.

When he managed to get his eyes open properly, he saw that the room wasn't swinging around him; the lighting was. More, he wasn't in an actual room, as he had first thought: it was more of a space that appeared to have been chewed out of the bowels of the Facility, strung with lines of emergency glow-stick that swung gently back and forth in an inconstant gust of air that was distinctly...unsavoury.

"What did you do to the Facility?" he demanded, falling back against a rough, uncomfortable surface behind him.

"Technically, we ain't done nuffink," said the little girl in front and slightly to the left of him. She prodded his head with one finger, straightening him as he tilted a little too far to the left. "This place is kinda a...leftover thing. Be a lot worse if we didn't do summink about it, too!"

"I don't know what that means," Bell said. "But if you think you're going to get a ransom for kidnapping me—"

"We didn't kidnap you," said a male voice, and Bell looked to his right to see a short man limp closer. "We just wanted you out of the way."

"You're Marx, I believe," said Bell. An awful suspicion overtook him. "Did you—you were the cook last night, weren't you?"

"I don't cook," said Marx, without blinking. "It turns out badly."

"*Flamin'* bad!" Kez said, grinning.

That grin told Director Bell all he needed to know.

"You *poisoned* me!"

"Wot you talkin' 'bout?" Kez asked cheerfully. "Got ta experience the real Tamoan curry, didden ya? Flamin' good, wasn't it?"

Director Bell stared at her. "He put actual Tamoan curry leaf in the dish?"

"Very authentic," Marx advised him. "Very high end. You don't get to eat that every day."

"No, because we don't have cast iron stomachs! Only the older Third Worlders still eat that!"

"Wot you still fussin' for, anyway?" demanded Kez. "Feelin' better, ain't ya?"

"Feeling *better*—?" But Bell had to stop and acknowledge that he was, in fact, feeling better. Had been feeling better since he regained consciousness, if one didn't count the splitting headache, which was new.

"What did you do to me?" he demanded.

"That's nice," grumbled Kez. "Fix a bloke's gut, and 'e still bellyaches."

"You're the ones who poisoned me!"

Kez looked at Marx. "Carries on a bit, don't 'e?"

"I assume," said Bell, refusing to rise to that bait with the rather wild determination that he was a grownup and above arguing with what appeared to be a twelve-year-old, "that you have a reason for kidnapping me."

"Yeah," said Kez. "You got in the way."

"I *beg* your pardon?"

"The sign does say *out of order*," Marx reminded him. "We were busy. You shouldn't have interrupted."

Alarmed, Director Bell demanded, "Interrupted what?"

"Ain't no fun if we tells ya," Kez said reproachfully. "Don't worry; we're just gunna keep you tied up for a bit, orright?"

Aware of a distinct trend in the wake of Kez and Marx's adventures, Director Bell swallowed. "You're not...you're not trying to blow up the Facility, are you?"

Kez's eyes lit up, and Marx said absolutely, "No. And you can stop arguing about it, Kez."

The little girl deflated slightly, and drummed her heels against the wall casing.

"If you're not trying to blow up the Facility—"

"That's the problem with you fringe WAOFy blokes," said Marx, conversationally. "You're always out to terminate problems and liquidate others, so you think everyone else thinks like you. You're a problem to us, but blowing you up isn't a good way to solve that problem—no, *pipe down*, kid, it's *not*."

Bell wondered if he'd imagined the mutter of "yeah, but

it's *fun*", and hoped so. "We're not trying to liquidate you," he said.

"Garbage," Marx said, without mincing matters. "You can't tell me there isn't a *kill if unable to detain* order on both of us. You and Time Corp, both."

"We always," Bell said stiffly, "endeavour to capture without injury. Up to a point. I should add that it was badly advised of you to poison me."

"Yeah," said Kez. "Special, *ain't* ya?"

Bell stared at her, wondering what she knew. "I'm not regular WAOF, if that's what you mean."

"Yeah, we figgered. Don't go stickin' yer nose up; we ain't here for you. Got *ovver* stuff to do."

"No one other than someone connected with Time Corp or the WAOF would try to bargain with Uncle Cheng," said Marx coldly. "Incursion Specialists is what you call yourselves, isn't it?"

"I have absolutely no idea what you're talking about," Bell said, with finality. "I'm part of a fringe group of the WAOF, but we *are* an official group. And we here at the Facility have no agreement with Uncle Cheng or any other lollymen."

"Yeah, not *'ficially*."

He sent a look of dislike in her direction. "I was trying to point out that your decision to kidnap—"

"Coo! Uses an out-of-order loo and reckons *we* kidnapped *'im*!"

"—your decision to harass—"

"Didn't *ask* ya to come in, did we? *Out of order*; said it real nice and clear."

The Director ground his teeth. He had no love for Marx, and no particular desire to have the man take control of the situation, but he found himself with a lingering regret that he had to deal with Kez as a result of that reprieve.

"Oi," said Kez. "Before we get rid av ya, listen up. You lot best be checkin' what your friends are up to, savvy?"

Bell stared at her. "Exactly what do you mean by that?"

He very much disliked the threat of violence, and he liked being accused of collaborating with Uncle Cheng even less, but the tenuous relationship the Incursion Specialists had with Uncle Cheng could be termed a very odd kind of friendship.

"Well," she said, "you ain't exactly 'appy wiv 'im, is ya? 'E's not real 'appy with you, either, far as I can tell."

"If you're suggesting that person or persons unknown—"

"Yeah, but they *ain't* unknown," Kez said. "That's the point. And they're makin' things pretty flamin' dangerous around the universe."

"The Incursion Specialists," said Bell, very, very carefully, "are not connected with Uncle Cheng and the lollymen in any official capacity whatsoever."

"Yeah, but they're pretty useful when it comes to stuff you don't wanna get yer own hands dirty wiv, I reckon," Kez observed. "They ain't 'zactly stayin' clean on their own account, though, see? An' every time you give 'em a spare bit o'fuel—"

"They raid the mess hall as well," finished Bell. "I'm aware of the proverb, thank you very much."

"It's wot you ain't aware of bovvers me," Kez said frankly. "Reckon you might want to ask your friends 'zactly wot they fink they're doin', messing wiv Fixed Points."

Bell felt as though the air had been driven from his lungs. It was true that there was a species of agreement between his part of the WAOF and Uncle Cheng—it was likewise true that his team had been investigating a distinct twisting of the universe lately—but it had never occurred to him that Fixed Points had actually been interfered with by Uncle Cheng or anyone else.

Again, this time in more of a strangled tone, he asked, "Exactly what do you mean by that?"

"Look around, bucko," said Marx. "Funny kind of room, isn't it?"

"Rather odorous too."

"That's 'cos there's a nice liddle cut-out where the sewerage goes," Kez told him. "This bit ain't here, though."

"I can see it's not here," retorted Bell. "We're sitting in it."

"Yes, but it wasn't originally a space," Marx said grimly. "It used to be a bit of the foundations. This was eaten away when the universe started to fall apart—or *will* start to fall apart."

"I beg your pardon?"

"No need to worry; we fixed it. But there are little reminders around the place, here and there. That's what your friend Uncle Cheng did, coming after us."

Bell very nearly winced, and managed to restrain himself. Uncle Cheng had promised to provide information leading to the capture of the two miscreants currently holding him captive, in return for which a blind eye would be turned to certain business transactions that came into the purview of the Incursion Specialists.

Trying to change the subject to one less dangerous, he asked once again, "What are you doing here today? If you're not going to blow up the Facility, what are you hoping for?"

"Nothing too much," said Marx. "Just a bit of movement here and there."

"Up an' down," agreed Kez. She nudged Marx with one elbow that must have been needle sharp by the wince he gave. "'Bout time, ain't it?"

Bell, resigned to the faintly plaintive sound to his voice, asked, "Are you going to hit me on the head again?"

"An' people say you're thick!" said Kez admiringly.

"I *beg* your pardon?" Bell said, stunned. Much to his own annoyance, he couldn't help saying, "People say—who says I'm stupid?"

"Don't worry 'bout it," Kez said, patting his arm.

Bell would have thought she was trying to comfort him if he hadn't felt the pull of unconsciousness tugging at him a moment later. He peered down at his arm and saw a small patch of something he strongly suspected was Drop-spot glistening there—just enough to knock out an average-sized man.

He tried to protest, ridiculously, that he had been expecting a hit in the head, but his legs gave up at the same time his tongue did, and he collapsed with his mouth still open. It seemed as though he was falling into a deep pit, softly and gently.

A voice wafted after him. "Better than bein' hit in the head, ain't it?"

Director Bell awoke again to find himself in a place he knew very well. Blue walls, cherry-wood conference table—this was the fourth conference room. Someone had pushed three chairs together and laid him across them. He was untied, but he was not alone, and even prone as he was, he could see that his comms badge was across the table. If he could get to his feet without falling over, he wouldn't be able to reach it before Kez or Marx got to it. The walls of the room, he knew, were soundproof.

And, realised Bell, his stomach sinking, from this room, it was easy to access the Core.

"What have you been doing while I've been asleep?" he demanded, panic rising in his chest. He sat up carefully, and rose just as carefully. "What did you—did you access the Core?"

"Don't get yer knickers in a twist," advised Kez. "It's better if you don't know what we was up to while you was asleep."

"I wouldn't try that, either," Marx said.

Bell, made aware by the significant glance the man shot him that he was clenching both of his fists, carefully released them.

"Right," said the man. "Listen up, because we haven't got much time. I just checked our Fixed Points, and they're looking pretty solid, but—"

Bell felt rather dazed. "*Our*—Fixed—Points?" Good heavens, they *knew* about the Fixed Points that were attached to them? How?

Marx grinned, and to Bell it seemed that for a moment he looked just as feral as Kez. "There are about five or so linked to us," he said. "And I'd *very strongly* advise against doing what

Uncle Cheng just attempted, because we've double-fixed those Fixed Points, and our science man is pretty sure that you'll make a much bigger mess of the universe this time if you try it again."

"Your science man...?"

"Ain't your business!" Kez shot at him, kicking him in the shin.

Bell gasped, but managed not to shout. He also retained enough pride not to bend and grasp the injured leg.

"Careful," Marx said to him. "Sometimes she bites, and I haven't had her disinfected lately."

Bell edged back just slightly, his calves hitting against the edge of the chair he'd just vacated. "There's no need to get violent—"

"*There's* some cheek!" scoffed Kez. "As if we ain't always tryin' to run away from Time Corp and you lot! *And* you let some mucker wiv a bunch of lollymen break Fixed Points around the place: *he* don't care about bein' violent!"

"We were not aware of the extent of Uncle Cheng's actions," Bell said stiffly.

"You're tellin' *us*," grumbled Kez. "Why'd you fink we 'ad to go an' fix 'em ourselves?"

"All citizens of all worlds are both permitted *and* encouraged to make reports to the WOAF or Time Corp if they should suspect—"

"And no doubt you or they would have encouraged us into one of your time-locked cells if we'd attempted it," Marx pointed out.

"Anyway," said Kez, in a congratulatory kind of way, "you figgered some av it out all by yourselves! We're just givin' you a bit av *'elp*, see? Lettin' you know who it was wot done it."

Bell eyed her in some dislike. "We're the Incursion Specialists. Of course we know something of the troubles around the universe: the two of you have been making chaos through time and space for as long as we can tell."

"Pro—pro*lific*, ain't we?"

"Unfortunately so," he said, without any abatement of dislike. "You've also made it quite hard for us to keep track of changes—or to classify them as major or minor, by the way."

"You blamin' *us* fer this!"

"Every time I turn around you're out and about in the universe, making trouble!"

"We clean up after ourselves," said Marx, shrugging. "Unlike your friends."

"I will reiterate once more that Uncle Cheng is no friend of mine. He's more friendly with Time Corp than I would prefer, but it's unlikely that my superiors will ever agree with me while he keeps bringing in the kind of money he brings in."

"Shoulda gorn into drug runnin'," said Kez morosely to Marx. "Coulda bought off Time Corp. Save us always runnin' around an' stuff."

"With what you can do, no amount of money would be enough to buy off Time Corp," Bell said, without mincing matters. "Or us, for that matter. We're interested in money—it's a necessity, after all—but we're also interested in advancements, and everything you do could be considered an advancement."

"Ain't my fault," the girl said irritably.

Bell said blankly, "*Fault*? We're not trying to punish you for your skills, we're trying to find out how to replicate them!"

"Yeah? An' I reckon you'd 'ave to lock me up to replicate 'em and all."

"There would be a certain amount of scientific study needed," Bell allowed.

"Yeah? Know where you can stuff that scientific study—?"

"Calm down, kid," said Marx, grabbing her by the back of the collar before she inflicted on Bell's shins the damage he was quite certain she was about to inflict.

The director cleared his throat and tried to pretend that he hadn't taken a few, swift steps sideways and then backward. "I'm not saying that I, personally, would do it—"

"But you wouldn't stop anyone else doing it," Marx finished

for him, with a smile that was just a little too cold and grey. "You company boys are all the same, no matter how deep you get into the centre."

"The world needs to be kept safe from chaos and unpredictability," said Bell defensively. "There are always sacrifices that need to be made in order to do so."

"Sacrifice yourselves, then," Kez advised him. "You lot 'ave got a *very bad 'abit* of tryin' to sacrifice me and I don't like it. Next time I'm gunna poke you in the eye."

Director Bell made a mental note to switch from his corrective implants to the old-fashioned but currently trendy glasses when he finally managed to escape from this unfortunate situation.

"You're lucky," Marx told him. "She told the last bloke she was going to bite his eyeball."

The director stared at the tiny girl in horror. He didn't doubt she would carry through with such a threat. He also didn't doubt that said eye would need disinfecting should it survive the assault.

"You said you weren't here to kidnap me," he reminded them both.

"Neither we did," Kez said. "Oi."

"What?"

"What's the time? LRT?"

Bell checked his timepiece. "Noon. Why?"

"That should do it," said Marx, exchanging a glance with Kez. He pointed at Bell. "You should be grateful that we didn't mess this place up. And do something about Uncle Cheng before he breaks the universe again."

"Don't worry about Uncle Cheng," said Bell, rather dourly. Noon. He needed to remember noon; he needed to find out what would happen, or had happened, today at noon. "We'll... deal with him in our own way."

"Yeah," said Kez, "but you prob'ly better listen a bit longer so you knows the right time an' place to get a good hold av 'im, yeah?"

There was a moment of silence, galling and strained. At last, through his teeth, Bell asked, "When would you suggest that we...approach...Uncle Cheng?"

"I'm glad you asked," said Marx affably. "I've got a nice little pre-programmed location scout here."

He waved it at Bell, who said absolutely, "I am *not* connecting that to my mains!"

Kez gave a rude snort of laughter. "Wot, you reckon we've put a liddle worm or summink in there to wriggle into your computer?"

"Yes," said Bell, without mincing words.

"Get your boys to turn it inside out, then," said Marx. "You should be able to get the co-ordinates without linking it to a mains system."

"You can be sure I'll do so," Bell warned.

"Reckon you're gunna have to make a Fixed Point out av it, too," Kez advised him.

"I'm aware," Bell said, still through his teeth. He would certainly make sure he knew what they had been up to in his Facility first, however.

"Orright," said Kez. "Reckon we'd best be orf, then. We're done, ain't we, Marx?"

"Finished up while he was asleep," Marx said, nodding.

"I want to know what you were doing in my Facility!"

"Too bad," said Kez. "C'mmon, Marx. This bloke's gettin' a bit antsy."

"I'll be seeing you again," Director Bell said threateningly.

"But not," said Marx, with his most unamused grin, "at a Fixed Point. That would be very unhealthy for the universe as we know it."

"I'm aware," said Bell. "But should we meet again outside a Fixed Point—"

"Yeah, yeah," muttered Kez. "*You'll* try an' grab us an' *we'll* chuck you into a black hole or summink."

"Is that a threat?"

"Wot *you* fink?"

"Don't bait the Incursion Specialists," Marx told her, and grabbed her hand.

"Oi! 'Ow come you can bait 'em and I'm not allowed—"

And they were gone.

Right in the middle of a sentence, they disappeared. Bell had heard of what Kez could do—theorised about how she could do it—but it was something else indeed to see it in real life.

He dropped back down into one of the conference seats to get his breath back, dizzy and more traumatised than he'd expected, then resolutely got to his feet once more, snatched up his comms badge, and said crisply, "All personnel to the blue conference room, *now*."

Bell's lieutenant said in disbelief, "How did they even get *in*?"

"I'm more worried about what they were doing here," said Bell.

"Well...weren't they trying to kidnap you, sir?"

"They had every opportunity to get me out of there without trouble," Bell said. "It wasn't about kidnapping me. I don't even think it was about talking to me, though they certainly took the opportunity."

"This is the sort of thing I was talking about, sir," the lieutenant said. "We can't predict them! Do you want us to go after them? I've made a report and uploaded a possible trajectory, but—"

"Send it to the *Slider*: let Captain Mikkel deal with it," said Bell. There were more pressing issues at play than chasing two aberrations who would likely never be caught.

"If we don't think he's going to catch them, why do we keep sending him after them, sir?"

"Because they seem to think he's playing with them, and there's less chance that they'll do personnel a mischief when he's the one chasing them."

"I heard they bit several of the officers."

"Only one of them did, and they didn't *kill* anyone, which is the point. We can always disinfect people, but it's hideously hard to get the right clearance to bring someone back to life once their timeline is listed as extinct in the Core. We can go back and do it, but the paperwork isn't worth it."

Director Bell paused and brooded about that for a moment, because in order to fix the mess that Time Corp and the WAOF had apparently caused by their casual friendship with Uncle Cheng, he was going to have to do a great deal of paperwork.

Director Bell didn't care for paperwork, but he cared even less for the immense mess left behind when someone changed things in the Core without the appropriate paperwork. The whole of the Twelve Worlds and their timelines might as well be run by anarchists. Paperwork might be a pain in the derrière, but it was also all that stopped a society from slipping over the edge into savagery.

"It's time to find out where Uncle Cheng is," he said. "Time Corp isn't going to like it, but they won't object once they know the reason. In the meantime, tell me *everything* that happened at noon today."

ATTN: DIRECTOR BELL, THE FACILITY

The following is the requested transcript from the surveillance recovered from co-ordinates previously given. Persons in the footage have been identified as Uncle Cheng and hunter-for-hire Vladivostok. In the footage we see Uncle Cheng returning to his private quarters and removing his overcoat as a hunter sits in the shadows beside the windows. Uncle Cheng loosens his cufflinks and then stops. He has seen the hunter by the window.

Transcript:

UC: I didn't order a hunter.

Hunter: I come on the orders of another.

UC: *(laughs, removes cufflinks)* You're a little out of your depth, I believe. Do you know who I am?

Hunter *(moving forward, knife in one hand)***:** Uncle Cheng. Patriarch of the Cheng family, master of the Blue Boy Lollymen—

UC: If you know who I am, you should know that you're making a rather unfortunate mistake right now.

Hunter: No. You made a mistake.

UC: I do warn you that should you go through with your contract and kill me, you will be hunted through the length and breadth of the known worlds by the WAOF and Time Corp combined.

Hunter: I will not be hunted.

UC: There is something you should know before you kill me.

Hunter: I know the hunt. I know the cost of my employment. I know the terms of my employment. I do not wish to know anything else.

UC: Wait. Then tell me who employed you.

Hunter: I was given orders from Director Bell.

UC: You don't know the whole of it. Your employer will want to talk to me. The Incursion Specialists will want to know that Marcus Solomon is alive!

Hunter: I have no orders to wait for speech. My employer does not wish to speak with you: that is why I am here.

UC: I am the only one who knows how to make his timeline extinct again. No one but myself can recover the Fixed Point that's about to break now that he knows when he dies.

Hunter: That is not my concern. Will you run?

UC: I can offer you ten times what they paid you to kill me.

Hunter: I have enough money. Will you run?

UC: I can offer—

Hunter: There is nothing you can offer me. Will you run?

UC: I refuse to run.

The footage then shows a confirmed kill. Should we proceed with further investigations? Early indicators in the Core do seem to suggest an extinct timeline coming back, as well as the early markers of disintegration of a Fixed Point if that timeline is not returned to an extinct reading. Please advise.

INCURSION SPECIALISTS INTERNAL MEMO

ATTN: DIRECTOR BELL

On checking the Facility's records for today, it appears that you were in three places at one time during the course of the day. That, combined with the presence of some species of universal rot in the foundations, makes it impossible for us to investigate the hour between eleven and noon LRT as it would destabilise us to the point of an incursion that could create a Fixed Point. Please advise as to how you would like us to proceed.

Investigations Unit, Member Johansson